CODE NAME: SPIRIT

COLONEL DON WILSON

WESTBOW·
PRESS
A DIVISION OF THOMAS NELSON
& ZONDERVAN

WestBow Press books may be ordered through booksellers or by contacting:

WestBow Press
A Division of Thomas Nelson & Zondervan
1663 Liberty Drive
Bloomington, IN 47403
www.westbowpress.com
1 (866) 928-1240

ISBN: 978-1-4908-3281-4 (sc)
ISBN: 978-1-4908-3282-1 (hc)
ISBN: 978-1-4908-3280-7 (e)

Library of Congress Control Number: 2014905917

Printed in the United States of America.

WestBow Press rev. date: 04/15/2014

DEDICATION

To the most distinguished citizens of all, better citizens than I, the many brave men and women who sacrificed their lives on foreign soil for an America different than the one we have today, because their elected countrymen, older and wiser, for whatever reasons asked them to lay their lives on the line. Was their sacrifice in vain? America has changed over the years. Human behavior tolerated today was thought criminal in the past. Sadly many elderly veterans look at our nation of today and say, "This is not the America I fought to protect." To honor old friends, no longer with us, I have used some of their names in this fictional story because each in his or her own way had a hand in shaping my life.

TABLE OF CONTENTS

This fictional book recounts the continuing career of a remarkable man in secret service to his country, code name: WILLIAM TELL which for security reasons later changed to code name SPIRIT. Looking back over an army career spanning twenty-three years and two wars, I feel justified in espousing a particular point of view concerning the use of armed force. The first and foremost consideration is the fact that there is nothing more important than the dignity and value of a single human life. A commanding officer once told his men prior to a proficiency test that without enthusiasm for one's work, a soldier is dead from the neck up and soon will be dead--*period*. Therefore, in the service we emphasize and promote *esprit de corps*. That, coupled with training, just cause and good leadership, *is* an awesome combination.

Few leaders choose a military career because they love a good fight. I have never known a leader who didn't regret the tragic loss of blood. I've seen commanders shedding tears over casualty reports. Through the centuries, the profession of arms has attracted the brilliant, the loyal, the stupid and the egotistical looking for a measure of immortality by carving a niche in history through generalship. And there are those few who are simply intrigued, fascinated and, yes, stimulated by the study of armed conflict. The best are guided by the motto of the United States Military Academy at West Point: "Duty, Honor, Country." History tells us of men with the warrior's spirit, like Stonewall Jackson who just before a major action turned to an aide and described his feelings at the moment as "delicious excitement." General Robert E. Lee is said to have commented when surveying a bloody battle's aftermath, "It is well that war is so horrible. We would grow too fond of it." In today's America there are few responsible men who would fight for the glory of it. The professional soldiers I have known and lived among consider themselves a deterrent to war and regard the military as an honorable vocation, a way to serve their country which offers constant challenge, agreeing with an acknowledged warrior, General George S. Patton, who said, "Compared to war all other forms of human endeavor pale to insignificance." However, while the study of war is both fascinating and necessary for preparedness, the actual fighting should be avoided where possible. But, if unavoidable, have Plan B ready. And we must never forget that wars have started because *one* side believed the *other* would not fight, or it would be a conflict of short duration. Wars always cost more than expected.

The history of our nation's military shines with stirring chapters in the application of righteous might to preserve and protect our Constitution and the American way of life. Conversely, there were occasions when the best intentions to continue this noble heritage were perverted and overtaken by disaster, with its bitter aftermath of disillusion. As a people, we are not very good students of history; we keep repeating the same mistakes at dreadful cost. The professional soldier is the exception. He studies diligently military history and learns much from it. Fresh in the memory of our adult population but being ignored in our schools is our recent involvement in Southeast Asia. Here, in effect, we patted the South Vietnamese on the head and said, "Step aside, boy. We'll handle this." Some of our best generals advised "This is the wrong war at the wrong time with the wrong enemy." but political considerations overrode good sense. The end result recalls to mind a seemingly appropriate epitaph by Rudyard Kipling, "Here lies an Englishman who tried to hustle the east.

Evil exists to provide the necessary conflict in this life, which shapes the character of us all as individuals and as nations. In this respect, life is a game, a test. Looking back over our recent conflicts, one may fairly ask, "Why is being good so costly?" Let it not be written that in human and economic terms America was bankrupted by war or that America was destroyed by leaders who, by engaging in war, became an evil in themselves by seeking power or a loftier place in history.

Considering that since the end of World War II we have been dealing with an unreasonable and dogged adversary who plays by only one rule--the end justifies the means--any rational person would have to agree that over the years our government has done a reasonable job countering communist aggression—Vietnam being the exception. We have done this by side-stepping the UN superpower's veto. There is no last word in diplomacy. We have done well when we have exercised it and poorly when we have not. Despite a public clamoring for the president to do something, many times the precise thing to do is nothing. Over the years effective covert action has stalled Soviet aggression and contributed in no small way to force Soviet thinking inward to solve growing domestic problems and to finally begin restructuring their society and warming the chill of the Cold War.

Although fictitious, this is a story of *possible* continuing efforts which could have secretly aided in bringing us to where we are today in our relations with Russia. It also suggests that we continue to search for effective ways beyond the usual to prevent escalation of incidents into a general conflagration. We cannot stand by watching the evil of this world close in around us until it's too late, and we stand alone and eventually become cursed by the enemy within—ourselves. It is not a question of *if* we are to play the game. We *must,* so let us play to win by using our imaginations to conceive methods which achieve our noble goals with the least expenditure of our precious human and material resources. This is a story of leaders who tried to do just that. This is a story of winners.

CHAPTER 1

PAST IS PROLOGUE

As I said in my first report, *Code Name: WILLIAM TELL*, I was researching material for a new book and began probing into areas I didn't comprehend, and making people in high places uncomfortable. To understate the alarming fact, I had struck a nerve at the top. Please excuse me. Allow me to introduce myself. I am Lieutenant Colonel Donald "Scoop" Coward, U.S. Army, retired, and since my retirement I have authored several military history books.

Although I had a top secret security clearance, it didn't mean I had a need to know. Nevertheless, as a writer with a lead to follow, a need to know was gnawing at my gut. On the thinnest of clues, a curiosity became an obsession that grew stronger with each new exposure in my research. Had I known early on that the information I unearthed was classified top secret, I would have dropped the subject, but in time it became too late. I had learned enough to be intrigued beyond my ability to back off.

The trail narrowed to one mysterious and shadowy figure whose veiled activities were highly successful in spite of being hampered by precious little intelligence and only rudimentary information about the situation into which he would be placed. He would have to assess the situation on the ground and concoct a scheme to succeed in his mission using his highly developed imagination and sheer audacity as circumstances developed before him. He was not a super-hero yet--just a man faced with difficult situations that required quick, on-the-spot decisions and fast action to create a situation his enemy would fall into believing their misfortune was entirely accidental. I thought, *nice trick if you can do it.*

My search for this man's service record took me to my friend and colleague, the chief of army military history, who had assisted me many times in my work writing military history for public consumption. It was here that I collided with the solid wall of secrecy I hoped to penetrate in the person of Brigadier General Albert J. Betancourt, whose friendship allowed me to call him "Court." He had held that post longer than any of his predecessors. I wondered why he would stay so long in a position most officers considered a backwater of army assignments. Soon I would learn why.

When I asked to see the service record of Captain Hunter William Bowman, Court took a serious, almost unfriendly attitude and told me not to meddle in something that was none of my business and to find another obsession. This only confirmed my suspicion that Bowman was the man I sought and there was a cover-up in place. I continued to press Court for answers, knowing he'd understand what happens to a writer with a hot lead he couldn't drop. Finally, Court told me to wait a few days--that he had to talk to some people. "Some people" turned out to be the top of the chain of command, beginning with the commander in chief himself, who had inherited from a previous president an organization as secret as the Manhattan Project of WWII--a foreign affairs tool with an impressive succession of Cold War victories.

My work has resulted in a good reputation as "The Soldier's Historian." Military history became my niche as a writer. I wrote from the point of view of the average soldier rather than strategic considerations. I hoped it would cause the powers that be to carefully consider the human aspects of sending the cream of our young generation into harm's way. I once heard an historian say, "As good men become killed in action, it increases the percentage of bad guys at home." To put it as simply as I can, in sending our youth into the meat grinder of war, we must have an affirmative answer to the all-important question, "Are we on God's side in this?" If we, as our national motto states, truly trust in God, we must be careful to be sure we are doing His will. We can be certain of His blessing if we determine to fight what is evil in God's sight and not our own.

It was this personal approach that caused me to stumble unto Bowman, which started some discussion at the highest level on what to do about me. The president's decision was not only to bring me into the tiny inner circle of secrecy but also to assign me duty as the historian of this secret organization with the warning that what I wrote was not for publication but locked away, hopefully for all of my lifetime. But, if the world situation changed for the better and the information could be declassified, I would have first rights to publish.

I soon learned that one day shortly after the Korean War, near the end of a lackluster term in office, a president in the solitude of the Oval Office found time to think of some way to brighten his tenure in office. He gave his imagination free rein. Soon an idea began to grow into a solution to a serious problem. It would be the closest-held secret since the atomic bomb. From this secret would come a remarkable man, code-named WILLIAM TELL.

I said the circle of secrecy was tiny, and indeed it was. The smaller the circle, the more secure the secret. To better understand the environment in which this body of remarkable men worked, it is vital that we understand the mission and organization of MOPS:

Military Operatives to Prevent Subversion

The MOPS Mission:

At the discretion and direction of the President of the United States, conduct covert anti-terrorist and anti-subversion operations in support of U.S. foreign policy worldwide. Such missions will be accomplished in a manner as to hold secret the existence of MOPS from the enemy and friendly governments alike.

The Chain of Command

President

Chairman, Joint Chiefs of Staff

MOPS Chief of Staff

Task Team Commanders (4)

Four teams to be tailored to the mission in terms of expertise, number of personnel, and equipment required.

The Code Names of Key People

The President: EVEREST (EV)

Chairman of the JCS: CLIMBER (CR)

MOPS Chief of Staff: WIZARD (WD)

Army Facilitator: MULEY (ML)

Navy Facilitator*: SWAB (SB)

Air Force Facilitator*: TALON (TN)

CIA Rep*: BLANKET (BK)

FBI Rep*: GANGSTER (GR)

Task Team Commander: MERLIN (MR)

Task Team Commander: SIDEKICK (SK)

Task Team Commander: VICEROY (VY)

Task Team Commander: WILLIAM TELL (WT)

MOPS Home Base: MAGNOLIA (MA)

*Note that these do not know of the existence of
MOPS but act on requirement priority K2.

Hunter William Bowman preferred to be called Bill. I suppose to the casual observer, there was nothing in young Bill's make-up that would signal coming greatness. But who knows what trigger lies deep in one's character that when pulled would fire his imagination?

As a teenager, beneath the surface in his private world, there were two overriding keys to his motivation of which he seldom spoke--his love of country and his deep Christian faith. His mother's influence gave birth to an abiding faith. He was raised in a service family, and his father's influence instilled love of country and a wish to serve it the best way he could. The "best way" brought him the respect and admiration of his superiors and subordinates alike. He was a leader because he wanted to be.

When he joined the army he qualified for officer candidate school (OCS), and after a maturation period of two and a half years as an enlisted man, Sergeant Bowman earned his commission as a Second Lieutenant. Serving as a rifle platoon leader during the Korean War, he was awarded the Distinguished Service Cross and the Congressional Medal of Honor. His performance of that duty was always beyond his superior's expectations. Even so, he didn't think much about it. He was sometimes surprised at his own performance, and he didn't try to explain it. Nevertheless, it could be attributed to his upbringing which reminds me of the Bible verse: Proverbs 22:6 "Train-up a child in the way he should

go and when he is old he will not depart from it." I'm sure Bill
was familiar with that one.

As a soldier and leader, Bill had set clear-cut goals and moved
toward them with the persistence of time itself. Let it not be said
there were no obstacles to overcome. When he was a boy, there
were plenty which could have discouraged any young man, but
Bill's positive attitude led him to accept whatever he could get and
build upon it, permitting him to overcome difficulties and inspire
others. It was while Captain "Bill" Bowman commanded a tank
company at Fort Hood, Texas that General Betancourt recruited
him for Top Secret service.

There was something strange about that interview. General
Betancourt thought he would need a powerful sales pitch to
convince Captain Bowman, a Medal of Honor winner with a great
career mapped out for him, to join the professional obscurity of
an entirely unknown organization. Instead, it was as if Bill knew
beforehand of his visit and its purpose, and quickly agreed to
serve. He soon learned he would fight a cold war of improvisation
conducted without rules by men of incredible imagination and
audacity. They were able to quickly accomplish the mission and
skillfully extricate themselves from potentially compromising
situations.

Prior to each mission we gave our operatives all the information
possible, but more often than not our team leader was forced to
assess conditions on the ground and formulate a plan for success—
improvisation indeed. The advantage of this type of carefully
crafted spontaneity is that the enemy has no foreknowledge of
whom or by what means they would be hit. All our actions,
even those developed on the spot, appeared to the enemy as
unfortunate—bad luck or the result of their own mistakes.

Team members were trained to translate the president's
mission directive into specific action. They were imaginative
enough to think outside the military box and clever enough to
inspire men who would risk their lives. Trainers seemed to have
a dislike for anything that smacked of decency in fighting. This

was war, and all is fair--fighting without rules. Fighting to kill is the only honest fighting there is. Dirty tricks are to be instinctive. They studied disguises, how to pass messages and other secret-agent tradecraft. Nonetheless, operatives were selected as much for their personalities as for their fitness. Teammates had to work well with each other and have a sense of humor, able to laugh off difficulties, knowing a little thought would provide an answer. Camaraderie would be as essential to the mission's success as fitness and field craft.

To put this power to fight into action, we must have a firm conviction, abiding faith and knowledge of where we came from and where we are going. Our God-given constitution begins, "We the People--" If we as a nation are led by men and women who couldn't care less what God thinks or who are ignorant of our Godly heritage, we are destined to fail. Mark Twain said the story of a nation is best told by her people. If her people are good they will prosper, but if they are bad they will fall.

Thomas Jefferson put it this way,

> God who gave us life gave us liberty. And can the liberties of a nation be thought secure when we have removed their only firm basis, a conviction in the minds of the people that these liberties are a gift of God, that they are not to be violated but with His wrath? Indeed, I tremble for my country when I reflect that God is just; that His justice cannot sleep forever.

Abraham Lincoln warned, "A nation of free men will live forever, or die by suicide." What did he mean? He meant that we are our own worst enemy. To ignore God is to become the enemy within who would cause our destruction. I don't mean to oversimplify, but in the beginning our Founding Fathers could not have created the pagan nation a large segment of our population has become because their formal education included a priority that is missing today, our Godly heritage. We can't afford to gamble on a better idea, because there is none. We take it from our Founding Fathers who were Bible trained from infancy that God is in control. Let me quote from President Jefferson once again, "The Christian Religion, when divested of the rags in which they (the clergy) have enveloped it, and brought to the original purity and simplicity of its benevolent institution, is a religion of all others most friendly to liberty, science, and the freest expansion of the human mind." Believing all this, I and my colleagues in MOPS are dedicated to do our work in the light of God's Word

CHAPTER 2

REASONS TO
CELEBRATE

U nderstanding something of Bill Bowman and his organization, I'll proceed with his remarkable story as I recorded it. MAGNOLIA was alive with celebration and good cheer. A man was dead--no eulogy and no memorial. Not just any man but a menace to the entire world, a man of whom the intelligence community of the free world knew little and feared much. For many years he was unidentifiable except by his code name KRAIT, meaning the deadly viper. All the principles in his demise were in attendance. CLIMBER and WIZARD were beaming with more than satisfaction. Task Team WILLIAM TELL had done it, and its leader, Major Hunter William Bowman, hereafter to be referred to by his code name, WILLIAM TELL, was feeling the pride of a leader whose subordinate had accomplished a great feat. All the men of MOPS were relieved that they would never again encounter KRAIT, the Soviet's KGB agent who could justly be called the devil's disciple. The honoree was

WILLIAM TELL's longtime friend and subordinate, Sergeant Major Billy R. Caruth, who had on two occasions refused a battlefield commission, but now was to be the recipient of a Captain's commission for doing what no one else in the free world's intelligence community was able to accomplish. He killed KRAIT. Henceforth, Sergeant Caruth, code number 38, will be referred to by a code name, MERLIN and will command his own Task Team, inherited from BUCKAROO who retired. Also called *ole' just in case*, MERLIN always had an alternate plan when in a tight spot—just in case. One of his alternate plans killed KRAIT.

At the celebration dinner it was recalled that KRAIT, under pressure, was tricked by MERLIN into stealing a booby-trapped Lysander aircraft which exploded in flight, killing KRAIT. Explaining the circumstances, WIZARD produced a document which the president received by diplomatic courier from the prime minister of Equatoria and marked for his eyes only. It was a bill for the destroyed Lysander and stamped "*Cancelled— paid in full*," and signed with grateful thanks. So KRAIT, the practitioner of a blood red evil, was relegated to the dust bin of history. Nonetheless, even dead, we would hear of him once more. WIZARD commented, "Now that KRAIT has left the stage, who will play the villain?"

* * *

After being recruited into MOPS, WILLIAM TELL's first mission was code-named OPERATION ARROW, which took him to the Republic of Tierra Blanca in South America. There he fell in love with his guide, a ravishingly beautiful widow named Antonia Lopez. Of course he was not aware she was a Soviet agent under the control of KRAIT. Nor was she aware that her husband had been killed by KRAIT. Bitter and disillusioned, she had traveled to Paris where she met KRAIT and was politically "reoriented" and joined the KGB to become agent SWALLOW. In that capacity she had become friendly with the American military attaché, Colonel George Morley, and under his influence began to see the error of her ways and vowed to make amends by rededicating herself to her country's service. She was well aware of KRAIT's ruthlessness and knew that the only way to separate from his control was to die. Yet maybe there was a way. First she would have to serve as a guide to a team from America assisting her government in resisting a coup instigated by Soviet backed Cuban insurgents supervised by KRAIT. In the process she became fascinated with the team leader, WILLIAM TELL. Soon her fascination became a love of what little she knew of him. Upon his departure, knowing she might never again see him, she extended an invitation to meet again in unofficial circumstances. The invitation took the form of a lingering and passionate kiss as well as a verbal encouragement to return to her soon.

Later, after completing a mission to the Middle-East, Bill found himself thinking often of that lovely lady he left behind and finally realized he, too, had fallen in love. He immediately phoned her and arranged a visit. Antonia felt his visit would not only confirm her feelings but enable her to fall in love with the rest of him, the part withheld from her because of the secrecy of his mission. Under instructions from KRAIT to learn more about the nameless man, she knew she had to protect him. She also knew she could not do that without arousing KRAIT's suspicions and he would quickly conclude that she would no longer be useful to him. This would not only be her death sentence, but she knew the method of her execution.

Bill was at home in his off-base apartment near the military complex, which sheltered MAGNOLIA. While on his return visit to Tierra Blanca, he had confirmed that his fascination had turned to love. Since that love was mutual, he sent a message to WIZARD requesting permission to marry, and was refused and directed to return at once. Bill was sure speaking to WIZARD face-to-face could convince him to grant permission. He phoned his folks and shared the good news and told them to be prepared to travel on short notice to attend his wedding. He was preparing to report to MAGNOLIA as directed by the recall message when the phone rang.

"Bill?"

"Who's calling?"

"George Morley from Tierra Blanca. Bill, I want you to get a hold of yourself. I hate to be the bearer of bad news, but--"

"What is it, sir?"

"Antonia--she' dead." Bill knew Colonel Morley's voice and took the news as fact, and therefore, the impact was immediate and devastating. Bill felt as if he had been struck in the face with a tremendous blow, and his legs could not support him as he struggled to find a chair.

"Bill, are you there?"

After a moment Bill responded in barely a whisper, "Yes George, what happened?"

"Bill, did you say something? I can't hear you."

"How'd it happen, George?"

"We suspect foul play Bill, but we cannot establish the cause of death. As far as the doctors can tell, she suffered a cardiac arrest, but she has no history of heart trouble. It was so quick. She felt no pain."

"That's a blessing. Have her folks been notified?"

"Yes. Bill, there is something very disturbing about all this. The circumstances were strange, so unlike Antonia. She was a very classy lady."

"What do you mean? What happened?"

"The scene of death was a sleazy greasy spoon bar and grill. You know what a nutrition nut she was?" Bill broke down and sobbed at the thought of Toni's existence in the past tense.

"Bill?"

"Yes sir?"

"You have my deepest condolences."

"Thank you, George. I appreciate that. Can you tell me more?"

"Well, yes, if you feel up to it. Strangely, they found her sitting in a booth in the back of the place, dressed in the vulgar clothing of a street walker. I found it hard to recognize her through the cheap make-up and brassy wig. The bartender said she was soliciting business from a farm worker in the back booth. I don't know what she was up to, and her government denies any knowledge of her activities since the coup attempt. Whatever she was doing, she was on her own."

"Have they got the farm worker?"

"No, he disappeared and no one can identify him."

"That's puzzling. What do you make of it?"

"We can only suspect that her unusual behavior is tied into another piece of information we have about her which until now we haven't given much credence."

"Oh? What's that?"

"When her husband's plane crashed she took the news very hard and took a trip to Europe to recover from shock. Quite naturally she sought solitude, but she dropped out of sight for nearly six months. When she resurfaced, according to friends, she had been transformed. There was hardness about her, and she became dedicated to her business...that's about it. We haven't much more to go on."

"Thanks George. You've been very considerate. If you learn any more please let me know. You might question her mother. She alluded to some difficulties of the last four years that might be of help."

Bill hung up, buried his face in his hands, and quietly grieved for his beloved Toni. He recalled his excited lovely lady so full of life and imagined-- or at least hoped--that he must have been a turning point in her life. He couldn't bring himself to believe she would hurt him. Besides, what did she know? If she was a professional, she knew enough to want to interrogate him further. Deep down he had the feeling she knew her life was in danger, and he wanted to believe she died protecting him in some way. The thought consoled him somewhat, but the burning questions remained: how was she killed and who did it?

* * *

Fast forwarding to about two months later, Bill returned from the successful OPERATION SNARE, the object of which was to kill KRAIT. By this time MOPS was aware of his favorite and ingenious weapon, the silent killer which left the assassin free of suspicion—colorless and odorless poison gas ejected from an innocent-looking cigarette lighter, leaving no hint of the cause of death but resulting in cardiac arrest. The gas dissipates upon contact with the oxygen in the air and is harmless in ten seconds but kills in only three seconds. Knowing this saved MERLIN's life.

The celebration of KRAIT'S death over, WILLIAM TELL returned to his bachelor apartment. Soon the desk clerk called, "Sir, there's a Colonel Morley to see you."

"Yes, send him up." Bill wondered why the Colonel was in Washington, all the way from Tierra Blanca. His head still buzzing he answered the knock at the door.

"Hello, George. Come on in and make yourself at home. What's up?"

"Bill, I can't stay long, so I'll come right out with it. Antonia's alive and well."

"What? Say that again." Bill asked in astonishment.

"Before I go into the details she wants to apologize for what she put you through. But now that KRAIT is dead, she can come out of hiding. She asked me to tell you the whole story before she asks your forgiveness."

"Ask my forgiveness?

"Yes, there is a lot more to the story than you know."

"Okay, go on."

"After you were recalled from your visit and flew home, she came to me for help."

"Help for what?"

"She was a KGB agent, code-name SWALLOW."

"What? That can't be. Are you sure?

"No doubt about it, but a position she came to regret about two years ago. After her husband's death she went to Paris grieving, bitter and confused, an easy prey for someone like KRAIT. She was politically "reoriented" and sent to the KGB Academy. Under KRAIT's control she returned to Tierra Blanca as a mole agent. Unknown at the time her friendship with me was calculated to obtain information prior to KRAIT's attempt at a coup. Eventually her feelings began to change, and she was ashamed of what she had been and done. She could not condone the brutal things being done in preparation for the coup attempt and came to me and confessed her part in it, offering to help her country in any way she could. We went to President Armandarez and supplied him with the information he needed to counter the coup. It was then she learned how her husband was murdered. Her husband got wind of the plot and quietly began to investigate. KRAIT, disguised as a mechanic, tampered with the oxygen system in his jet fighter, which caused her husband to black out and crash.

"During your three-day return visit after the coup attempt her feelings for you left no doubt that it was true love. Antonia, after long and deliberate thought, knew the only way she could separate from KRAIT was to die. She came to me with an idea, and together we cooked up a scenario that, although highly dangerous for her, would work. After you were recalled and flew home, we put the plan into action. She and KRAIT had set up a meeting place, a sleazy bar and grill in a poor suburb of the capitol city of Buena Vista. Both in disguises, he a farm worker and she a prostitute, they met to discuss the progress of her assignment to uncover information about the mysterious American—you. In her effort to protect you she purposely went too far, and KRAIT knew he could no longer trust her and produced the lighter to kill her. Expelling and holding her breath, she feigned death and slumped over in the booth. He slid out of the booth and quietly left her for dead. She waited until she was sure he was gone. Then feigning illness, she staggered to the bar and called me. For the information of those listening, she said she had an attack and to send an ambulance. I arrived with the ambulance, and playing the doctor, I pronounced her dead at the scene. We immediately ran the obituary in the newspaper, and then she laid low until news of KRAIT's death was confirmed by the CIA. Of course, Antonia's parents were part of the deception and handled her business. She asked me to explain everything before she dared approach you."

"George, you'll never know what a crushing blow your call was. And now you tell me she's alive. I don't know what to say except thank God."

"She told me to tell you her feelings for you as you know them have not changed. Every detail of your three day visit was genuine. Now, do you see why she asks your forgiveness?"

"Forgiveness could not be easier."

"I'm so happy for you both. Well, I have to catch my flight. I just received orders reassigning me to our embassy in Germany. My staff car is waiting downstairs."

"Lucky dog, I envy you your new job. I hate to see you leave so soon, but thanks for bringing the good news personally."

"Truly my pleasure, but I do have to run. I'd like to stay and celebrate with you. But I'm on a tight timetable, and duty calls. So long my friend."

Bill closed the door and leaned against it and began to sob with joy that his beloved Toni would be waiting to see him. He turned and sat down near the phone to call. As he picked up the phone, there was a knock at the door. He looked around to see if Colonel Morley had forgotten something, but no, so he went to the door and swung it open and beheld a lovely vision in white.

"Toni...Darling!"

"Hello my love. As I was saying our wedding can be spectacular by the pool with floating lights."

Bill stood momentarily frozen with astonishment. After a moment Toni whispered,

"Why are you looking at me like that? Aren't you going to ask me in?"

"I'm as stunned as I was at the news of your death. I see an apparition. How can a ghost be so lovely?"

"I'm no ghost—touch me my love."

In an instant they embraced in a long and passionate kiss.

"Toni, I never knew there was anything in life that could bring such intense pain as the news I had lost you."

"Poor dear, but it was the only way I could escape the situation with KRAIT. I had no idea how long I'd have to remain in hiding. The sixty-four days until his death seemed like an eternity. I longed for you so. I thank God when I think of how much longer it could have taken. I imagined our meeting again when we were old and gray. Knowing your reaction to the bad news, I lived in the hope you'd understand what had to be done."

"I do now. I recognize the risk you took and appreciate your imagination in a tough spot."

"In view of my background, the CIA will debrief me to learn all they can about KGB organization and operations. It won't be much, KRAIT kept all his agents in the field isolated from each other whenever possible."

"They will want to know the details of your training." Bill thought a bit and then instructed, "When they question you about the Tierra Blanca operation they will know about your part in quelling the coup and the assistance you gave me and my team, but remember, you never knew my name or the specific organization I worked for. Regarding your return, there are some people I must talk to. In the meantime, I think you should stay here with me. You can have my bedroom; there's a Murphy bed here in the living room for me."

"Still the Christian gentleman?"

"Dear, I long for the day I'll feel free to make mad, passionate love to you, but until the knot is tied, I feel I would not be able to function in that role. As they say, the most important sexual organ is the mind."

"As long as that's the only reason, I respect your integrity"

Playfully, Bill responded, "Besides, there's that red-head in Baltimore."

Toni, acting in kind, grabbed the nearest object and threw it at Bill.

"Wow, a direct hit. I'm glad it was a pillow."

"After all we've been through I wouldn't for the world want to hurt you again."

CHAPTER 3

SUSPICIONS

With KRAIT dead and Toni alive, Bill's world was back in balance. The celebration over, it was back to business, as unusual as it was. WIZARD summoned WILLIAM TELL to his office, closed the door, and surprised him with an unusual request.

"WT, wouldn't you agree that we have pretty much all we need here in MAGNOLIA; both for our comfort and mission requirements?"

"Pretty much, but there is one thing missing."

"Oh, and what would that be?"

"We have a need for spiritual guidance, Sir."

"You're making it easy for me. That's exactly why I asked you here. We are too small to rate a full time chaplain, and in this business you know we need one. Bringing in an outside chaplain would mean a security problem. We could not explain to him the specific nature of our need. I have had requests from team commanders to do something to remedy that omission. Furthermore, you figure in that request. It seems your faith is so evident that they'd like you to fill that void."

Holding up his hand to silence WT, he continued, "Before you answer, let me explain my vision of the job. First and foremost you are a Task Team Commander, and your additional duty as unofficial chaplain to MOPS will be as a spiritual counselor when needed at the request of individual team members. If you are asked to conduct a regular Bible study, participation must be voluntary and not to exceed one hour a week so as not to interfere with mission preparation. Okay?"

"I'd be honored, sir."

"Good, I need it as much as the men. One other thing, considering our mission, there are many examples in the Bible where God directed violence against the enemies of Israel and created miraculous assistance. Be sure to study those to emphasize we are on God's side, His instruments in fighting evil."

"I agree."

"Good. Now to change the subject, what about this woman you wish to marry?"

"This woman, as you put it, is Antonia Lopez, my guide during Operation ARROW who fell in love with me. Being a little slow on the up-take in this kind of situation, it wasn't until after ARROW II that it finally dawned on me that I also had fallen in love with her. I only just learned she was a KGB agent, code named SWALLOW."

" Yes, I know the whole story."

"You do?"

"Yes, Colonel Morley reported the facts to CLIMBER who had her picked up at your apartment today to interview her before her debriefing by the CIA."

"Sir, because of her experience, I hope our government won't want to put her to work as an agent, even if she offers."

"With KRAIT dead we already know she hasn't much to offer, so you needn't worry about that."

* * *

Elsewhere, in Moscow, Anatoly Kirishnin, sitting in his Kremlin office, contemplated a new and welcome development. KRAIT had finally met his match, and he felt safer now that his ambitious and evil agent was no longer a threat to his person and out of his hair forever. This pleasant circumstance occasioned a new look at his organization. He'd need a new superintendent of the KGB academy, and he'd need to select a new second-in-command. Of course, he knew he could probably not find a man with KRAIT's ability. But he had given it some thought over the last few months and in his heart he felt his less ambitious choice, no matter how proficient he might be, would downgrade the effectiveness of the KGB. KRAIT did cast a long shadow. This worried him because the recent failures in the field and KRAIT's death had disturbed his superiors in the Politburo who were pressuring him to turn over his duties to a younger man. He had for some time needed a victory, and now it was imperative. He was too old for field work, and the duties of office prevented his handling situations personally. He needed a talent for intrigue, a hard case who could handle tough situations with imagination and grit. In his search he examined the dossiers of all possible candidates with complete impartiality. After KRAIT's death Kirishnin was, for the first time, able to break open the secret file of agents known only to KRAIT. Individual files were destroyed when KRAIT murdered an agent. Therefore, SWALLOW's file had been destroyed. However, there was one dossier flagged with a memo which evidenced KRAIT's high regard of the agent. Kirishnin read the memo carefully. He had not previously considered a woman, but respecting KRAIT's judgment, he became intrigued with her exploits and resourcefulness. He appreciated the code name COUGAR because she seemed to take on the likeness of a dangerous predator. KRAIT had called her "The Iron Duchess" because she had been an aristocrat whose father assisted the revolution in the overthrow and murder of the Czar and his family. Furthermore, she was not only tough. She had the morals of an alley cat. Apparently, there was no situation she couldn't handle and enjoy doing so. She had a keen talent for extracting information from men under intimate circumstances. Like a female spider she was known to copulate and then kill the man if it suited the situation.

In two days of research Kirishnin settled on three potential candidates. After interviewing two he summoned COUGAR but she was nowhere to be found. There was no notation in her file that she was on assignment and her apartment had been vacated. Investigation shed no light on her whereabouts. Her disappearance was a mystery. Kirishnin had seen one or two similar situations and suspected her defection to the West.

* * *

Meanwhile, at MAGNOLIA, the MOPS briefing room buzzed with speculation. CLIMBER did not routinely participate in team briefings, but in this case he wanted to address the two available teams to explain the complexities of the current situation. He began, "Good evening gentlemen. I've called this briefing to make you aware of EVEREST's concern that the CIA has been infiltrated by the KGB. The CIA's internal security has launched an investigation to uncover the spy, but for the present all we know is the investigator could be the spy or a member of the investigating team. This fact is one of the reasons for the existence of MOPS. Working secretly and independently of the CIA and recruiting from the active service men of long and distinguished service in life threatening situations, we can be certain of our people and confident in their judgment in challenging situations. That and the fact that no one in the CIA has knowledge of MOPS leaves us free to complete our mission unimpaired by outside government agencies. Our carefully crafted wall of secrecy prevents even the CIA, including a KGB mole, from knowing we exist.

"As we understand our mission we cannot operate inside the limits of our borders. We leave that job to the FBI. But once a target leaves our country, he is fair game. So if a foreign agent is forced to flight, he can become our mission. I tell you this as general information, but it too is classified *top secret*.

"Change of subject. As time marched on our nation grew liberal to the extreme, and in this climate of political correctness, morals declined, bringing to mind the statement of Abraham Lincoln, 'Nothing is politically right which is morally wrong.' Tolerance is the last virtue of a declining society. We want to be oh-so-nice and offend nobody, even the liars. We first accommodate sin, then accept it, and then go so far as to teach it. Under this circumstance, I give our beloved country one generation or less to die as we know it, and all the brave men of generations past will have died for nothing. Our definition of a nice person and God's definition seem to be poles apart. All this affects the character--or lack thereof--of the new generation of leaders. In the words of George Washington, 'The people must remain ever vigilant against tyrants masquerading as public servants.' 'Elections, the object of which is ambition,' in the words of John Adams, 'I view with terror.' Candidates are not running to serve, but for financial security for the rest of their lives. I for one feel we must look carefully at the motives of any professional politician to prevent them from using the nation's secrets for political gain. It seems that today's definition of a smart politician is one who can see ways to circumvent the Constitution. Yes, civilian control of the military must be maintained. We cannot step in and try to change things ourselves. However, we must remain vigilant in order to know what's going on around us. If worse comes to worse, there may come a day when the only way left to save our nation and maintain our God-given freedoms is to step in temporarily with marshal law and apply The Uniform Code of Military Justice to our own Commander-in-Chief. These are critical times for our nation, but at present all we can do is watch and wait in the hope that the American people elect a responsible leader who will observe the letter and intent of our God-given Constitution."

"Speaking of politics, when I think of people whose political leanings are to the left or the right, I think of the passage in the Bible; I believe it to be Matthew 25:31.

> When the Son of Man comes in his glory, and all the angels with him, he will sit on his throne in heavenly glory. All the nations will be gathered before him, and he will separate the people one from another as a shepherd separates the sheep from the goats. He will put the sheep on his right and the goats on his left. Then the King will say to those on his right, 'Come, you who are blessed by my Father, take your inheritance, the Kingdom prepared for you since the creation of the world... Then he will say to those on the left, 'Depart from me, you who are cursed, into the eternal fire prepared for the devil and his angels.

"It is abundantly clear our new president's political leanings are left to the extreme and conflicts with our conservative Constitution.

"The key to this situation was recognized by EVEREST, the out-going president, who told us it would be wise to delay briefing the new president. He acts like a man with a superiority complex. It might be that as his administration assumes its character, we might decide to withhold from him all knowledge of MOPS. I am pained when I think this day should never come, but if it becomes clear that the elected president is as far left as we think, it could be disastrous for our nation and render it vulnerable to foreign subversion."

It was in this atmosphere that CLIMBER and WIZARD met in the privacy of WIZARD's office to discuss their mutual concerns about the newly elected administration and the cabinet appointments of the new president. CLIMBER spoke first, "I agree with EVEREST's concern over the probable reaction of the new president to a MOPS orientation."

"You felt that too, huh?"

"Yes, what are your feelings?"

"First, since you ask, who is he? By executive order he has frozen all record of his past. That alone should ring an alarm bell, but his statements taken beyond face value raise my suspicions. He is a politician and is practiced in political rhetoric which is intended to be vague and easily deceptive."

"Exactly, I see you and I are on the same page. We haven't yet shared with him our secret. However, he was apparently the people's choice, but personally I don't trust him. In our dealings with him we must be cautious and suspicious looking for possible hidden motives for his actions. We must more carefully examine the implications of his directives and advise him of perceived errors as affects the military. He may--and it is my hope--earn our trust. But when he says we are not a Christian nation, look out. That opens the door to all sorts of deviant behavior and political skullduggery. Frankly, I fear he has a secret agenda."

"Well, we shall see, but I fear his misuse of MOPS, not to mention its compromise."

The two admirals sat in deep thought for a few minutes, each giving the other time to consider their future conduct toward the new president. Finally CLIMBER said, "Enough said, this is a dangerous area of discussion. I just wanted to clear the air between us to be sure we think alike on this."

"I'm glad you did, sir. It's good to know I'm not alone in my doubts. And one other thing; I can't believe the citizen voters were in the majority. I think the illegal alien vote carried the election. That amounts to election fraud in my book. Who gave non-citizens and the dead the right to vote?"

"I guess we'll have to leave that question to the watchdogs. So, do we agree to take EVEREST's advice as an order and delay briefing the new president for the immediate future?"

"Yes, time will tell."

"That means with no mission directives coming from the new president we can put everyone on furlough."

"What do you think about keeping one team on standby and rotate the leaves so teams can study intelligence reports to keep abreast of the world situation and likely areas of deployment."

"That should cover unforeseen developments. Go ahead. The day may come when a situation develops which gives us no choice but to inform the president of MOPS."

"Of course, you understand that could cost us our jobs."

"Well, we were acting on the orders of a president still in office, and in the interim MOPS had been inactive."

WIZARD added, "I'll have ready a coded message on the call-in number to indicate we are active again and for teams to report back immediately. The coded message will be: SORRY, NO ONE IS AVAIABLE TO TAKE YOUR CALL, BUT IF THIS IS THE KIDS DADDY SAYS TO COME HOME NOW."

"Sounds very domestic."

CHAPTER 4

ANTICIPATION

Having been cleared by CLIMBER and the CIA, Toni's future had to be determined. Options both practical and out of the question were being discussed by CLIMBER and WIZARD. They decided that since neither MOPS nor the CIA wish to claim her services the question became whether or not to allow WILLIAM TELL to marry. WIZARD, knowing WT inside and out, felt that if he was really in love he must married the girl, secretly if necessary. In view of the facts that they both desired marriage, she was educated in America, held dual citizenship, she understood the secrecy of his job, had a career of her own and unable to have children, they felt their secret would be secure. They decided not to return WT to troops, but placed two conditions on their marriage—that it be a secret known only to the four of them and his and her parents, and the marriage must take place in Tierra Blanca. The army would know nothing of their marriage while he was a member of MOPs. They felt that was fair because of her wealth they would not need a family allowance.

The next day WILLIAM TELL was told of the decision, and understanding the need for secrecy, agreed to the conditions.

Being on leave as a result of the decision to delay the MOPS briefing of the new president, the timing could not have been more perfect. Bill hastened to inform Toni to plan the secret but spectacular wedding at poolside in the privacy of her walled-in hacienda. When he arrived back at his apartment, he found Toni up to her lovely neck in bubble bath. She wanted to rise and started to when Bill told her, "Venus, do not rise—I dare not tell you my news until you are dressed." He then departed the bathroom.

Toni mused...*How long can I stand this love at arm's length? I've a good mind to dry off and go to him in the buff. That would be fun...or would it? I don't want to shock the poor darling. Besides, to tempt him would be a sin.* Then looking up she said, "Lord give me strength."

Bill called from the living room. "Darling, what's keeping you?"

"Be patient dear. I didn't know when to expect you. Give me time to glamorize."

"Be careful you don't spoil what nature has already done."

Finally, she paused in the doorway, held out her arms and flew into his. Pulling back from a gentle kiss she said, "Okay, there's your tip, now what's the message?"

"Stingy tip. You'll have to do better than that."

"Naughty boy, are you sure you're ready for this?" At this her entire body became a passionate kiss. Bill reeled and his knees grew weak as he responded with all he could say,

"Wow!" Catching his breath and recovering his faculties, he said, "Darling, I have a persistent feeling we were made for each other."

"You know what they say, 'Great minds think alike'." Bill started to answer, but Toni interrupted, "The news, the news, what's the news?"

"My boss has ordered us to get married."

"Ordered us?"

"Yes, ordered because there are conditions."

"Oh, now what could be his conditions?"

"We are to marry out of the country... in secret, and the army is not to know about it. Let me add the marriage will take place in Tierra Blanca, poolside with floating lights and only your parents and mine present; and they must be sworn to secrecy."

"That'll work. Do we have to live in Tierra Blanca?"

"No, we can live here if you still want to move to your Atlanta office."

"As you know, I've been advised to do that. Now I have the deciding reason to move. I'll arrange for a condominium in Atlanta and you'll be my gentlemen friend."

"Sounds fine, however, I'll install a signal alert system to call-in from another location."

Alluringly, stroking Bill's cheek, Toni smiled and asked, "Very hush-hush, when's the wonderful day... and night?"

"We'll decide when I book Mom and Dad's flight."

"My love, it's so hard for me to think about our marriage and not dream about our first night in bed together."

"You're not alone in that thought, my dear, but I fear my ignorance will disappoint you, even though I've read a book on the subject."

"It takes more than head knowledge, my love. It takes practical experience and flaming emotions. That's where I come in. I'll be your teacher, your sex therapist. Your education shouldn't take too long. Just remember, in marriage intimate love making is the most fun two can share. Remember what the Bible says. My body is no longer mine but yours, and your body is mine. And we should never refuse each other except in mutual agreement or illness." Toni thought for a moment and added, "My wants and needs are as strong as yours, and I'll never feign a headache--end of first lesson."

"Good, I think we should postpone further discussion until the honeymoon."

"Okay, but not until we refer to the scriptures. I remember to tempt one to sin *is* a sin. Darling, where is your Bible?"

"Here. Why?"

"Turn to 1 Corinthians Chapter 7:1-5 and read it aloud." Bill began to read, "Now for the matters I wrote you about: It is good for man not to marry. But since there is so much immorality, each man should have his own wife. The husband should fulfill his marital duty to his wife, and likewise the wife to her husband. The wife's body does not belong to her alone but also to her husband. In the same way, the husband's body does not belong to him alone but to his wife. Do not deprive each other except by mutual consent and for a time, so that you may devote yourselves to prayer. Then come together again so that Satan will not tempt you because of your lack of self-control."

"See, do we agree without reservation with that scripture?"

"Of course, dear; the Bible is not some celestial salad bar where we can pick and choose what we like. It is our instructions from God for a happy life, and we must accept every word as truth."

"Good, then we have much to anticipate." Toni paused, then added, "I so look forward to acquiring your body."

"Is that all?"

"No...about half. Haven't you heard of the better half?"

"Yes, but not in that context, I can see now that frank communication is the key to a clear understanding of the other's needs, whatever they might be."

Later, with marriage preparations complete and only parents in attendance, the beautiful Tierra Blanca sunset heralded the intimate ceremony uniting Bill and Toni as one. Their Christian marriage vows promised total commitment to each other as long as they both shall live. Each felt God's blessing on their union. The honeymoon proved Toni to be a masterful teacher and for the first time Bill, usually quick to learn, tasted paradise as he truly appreciated God's Word that man should not live alone. Considering the intimacy of their relationship as an enduring gift to one another the couple soon became the lovers God intended.

CHAPTER 5

MORATORIUM

During MOP's moratorium much happened to justify
CLIMBER's concerns. WIZARD agreed that their
suspicions were well founded. The president's administration
had repeatedly violated provisions of the Constitution and
political skullduggery, bribery, and corruption were rampant.
The president's appointments to the Supreme Court packed the
court with extreme socialists who would back the president's
unconstitutional schemes with their seal of approval. It seemed
that a qualification for appointment to the Supreme Court of the
United States was to have a judge's decisions overturned many
times by a higher court.

America had become divided as never before in our history
and the culprit was ourselves, the enemy within. Congress had
created a utopia for themselves with a health plan, retirement,
and special privileges unavailable to the people. Congressmen and
senators would not kill the golden goose, and ignored attempts
to reform. Their salaries were way out of line for the service they
rendered.

The president's approvable rating sank to an all-time low. With the writing on the wall, even the media finally came to its senses and began to openly criticize the president and many of his cabinet members. Media honesty became the stimulant to encourage reform. They finally understood the comment by one of the signers of the constitution that "This document will only work for a God fearing people." Recently a Justice of the Supreme Court said our constitution is no longer valid and should be rewritten for the times. She didn't understand that it is not our God given Constitution that needs changing. It's the people who need to change. They took a lot of abuse, but the people had understood that they were not helpless and had taken enough to commence legal moves to take back their government from power hungry bureaucrats and professional politicians. The words of our fourth president, James Madison, rang true in the great majority of American hearts,

> Whenever there is an interest and power to do wrong, wrong will generally be done and not less by a powerful and interested Party, than by a prince. Wherever the real power of government lies there is danger of oppression. In our government, the power lies in the majority of the Community... government is the mere instrument of the major number of constituents.

During the wisely established MOPS moratorium sweeping changes had been initiated to remedy the crimes against the people and return our nation to an America recognizable to our Founding Fathers. The people finally realized that a talent for oration was present in all despots seeking power. They had forgotten another hypnotic orator named Adolph Hitler and his National Socialist Party (NAZI), which was to live a thousand years and died in twelve.

The president had actually done us a favor when he declared we were not a Christian nation and that prayer was a waste of time. This awaked the American people's spirituality and contradicted our national motto, "In God We Trust." Their ire aroused the people--through the legislatures of two thirds of the states--convened a constitutional convention to reunite our divided nation. Within eighteen months, according to Article V of the US Constitution, more than the required three fourths of the states had ratified the amendments, and they became the law of the land. This was one action the president had no power to veto. Now the people had regained the power that was rightfully theirs. A flat tax replaced the power and intimidation of the IRS. Annual income of less than $36,000 was tax free, and all other citizens without exception would be taxed at seventeen percent of income over that figure with no deductions—no loopholes. For example, seventeen percent of one whose annual salary was $1,000,000 would pay $163,880. The person who earned $50,000 would pay $2,380. The professional politicians were put on notice to find another job. Representatives were limited to three terms (six years) and Senators were limited to two terms (twelve years). Also congress could pass no law which would apply exclusively to themselves—unavailable to the people. Such laws in place were repealed. In addition, it prohibits government control of health care. Moreover, illegal aliens are not entitled to the rights of legal citizens, (i.e. welfare, Social Security, Driver's License and the vote). The Social Security Trust Fund may not be used for any purpose other than to pay benefits to citizens who contributed to it during their working years.

Citizen grand juries were convened, and indictments rendered against the president for crimes against the people amounting to treason against the United States of America. The president was relieved of office and tried and found guilty in a civil court because of a dysfunctional congress.

A general election was called to elect a new president and congress. The media, as a public service, which became the law of the land, allowed candidates a reasonable amount of free time for campaigning. Broadcast times were announced frequently to assure a well informed electorate and ratings were high. It forbade campaign fund-raising to keep special interests in their place. Term limits forced political parties to reform, and they held their conventions well aware of their responsibility to the people. All sitting candidates who were over the new term limits were ineligible for reelection. The United Nations was put on notice that we were a sovereign nation not subject to UN actions we deemed not in our interests. Funds allocated to the UN were discontinued and redirected to help pay down our national debt.

With a new president in office, elected by legal citizens, our nation was beginning again. For the present our people had learned a bitter lesson about selecting their leaders. Fast talking cons are usually successful by relying on a logical story line and not revealing their past history. The new president was open and honest about his qualification for the highest office in the land and his life story was an open book, thereby gaining the trust and confidence of the people. CLIMBER and WIZARD were impressed by the fact that he answered directly and completely questions put to him without sidestepping to avoid the issue. The previous president fended off tough questions to get back on the safe ground of what he was prepared to say and talked long enough to cause the viewer to forget the original question and be impressed with his eloquence.

Yes, the new president generated confidence, and as it turned out that confidence was completely justified. CLIMBER advised the president to leave two hours open on his busy schedule for a Top Secret briefing at a secret location. He was told not to wear clothing that would identify him as president and that he would travel incognito in an army helicopter, explaining that Marine One would attract too much attention. He would be met at the landing pad by Brigadier General Betancourt and quickly escorted to his office. In that way the president would attract no more attention than any civil servant.

CLIMBER sat alone at his desk thinking over the eight years. The crisis and problems which seemed without solution had been solved by extraordinary, but Constitutionally legal action by the people. Now somehow the ship of state sailed on as if it had a mind of its own, belying its need for a steady hand at the helm. Good government, after all, was a matter of public confidence. Anything which shook that confidence was to be avoided. While good management of all aspects of the nation's domestic affairs was mostly a matter of proficiency, foreign affairs were subject to all manner of unmanageable outside influences which had been the bane of existence for previous presidents, keeping them on the defensive and swamped in crisis after crisis. CLIMBER was confident in the new president's ability to take the initiative while keeping adversaries off-balance, chiefly owing to an idea and the resulting formation of a clandestine organization he was about to pass on to our new president. He thought of the Soviets as waging the Cold War, seizing every opportunity to further their goal of world domination spelled out in the Communist Manifesto. Where there was none, they sought to create the opportunity through subversion and manufacturing chaotic conditions which would cause citizens to be suspicious of government. CLIMBER thanked God and a former president's imagination that he now had the means of actively waging peace in the cold war arena with built-in plausible deniability should something go amiss.

He tried to place himself in the shoes of the new president when he would hear for the first time what had astounded other presidents years earlier. He asked himself some hard questions. How would the president react when the nation's best kept secret was revealed to him? Would he be reluctant to use this unorthodox tool or worse, misuse it and thereby render it useless? Perhaps he would, in what he believed to be righteous indignation, dismantle the organization out of hand. As no outgoing chief executive was available, CLIMBER must settle him into the idea with briefings on specific past successful operations. Moreover, he must provide the president with a complete picture of this secret organization so he would recognize opportunities for its use. No longer a fledgling, it now has a highly successful track record no one could deny. Perhaps this would overcome the natural inclination to delay deploying this important organization because of failure to recognize the opportunity.

From the oval office the president saw an army helicopter instead of Marine One ready to depart the White House helipad and tried to imagine the subject of the upcoming secret briefing. He hurried to the helicopter. The aircraft lifted off, climbed above the Washington Monument and turned toward the Potomac. He could see the reflecting pool and the Jefferson and Lincoln Memorials below. It looked as if he was going to Andrews Air Force Base, but the pilot flew wide of the landing pattern as the president wondered. Their destination became clear as the big chopper circled to set down with little notice at the Puzzle Palace on the Potomac, known to the general public as the Pentagon.

They were greeted quietly without the usual protocol and ushered quickly to the office of General Betancourt. In spite of the security measure, the commander in chief wondered why they had not been met by the chairman of the joint chiefs instead of a mere Brigadier. Several other questions needed answers and very soon, but for the moment he held his silence and did what he was asked. General Betancourt, turning to his secretary, ordered, "Hold all calls. The door to my office will be locked and don't expect us out for two hours or so."

Making eye contact, he asked, "Do you understand, Miss Bishop?"

"Yes sir, two hours at least."

As the MOPS historian I was responsible for recording this briefing. When he entered the General's office, the president located a seat and began walking toward it, but I redirected him toward the closet door saying,

"Just follow the General, Sir." The president witnessed the entry procedure with fascination as the General twisted the coat hanger rod backward, allowing the entire closet interior to swing inward to reveal a passageway. Arriving at a heavy soundproof door, he inserted a card in a wall slot where his face was scanned for identification. Upon opening the door, he quietly announced, "Gentlemen, the President of the United States!" One of the president's questions was answered when the chairman of the joint chiefs stepped forward to greet the two men.

Looking at his new Commander-in-Chief, he said, "I'm sorry, sir, I didn't meet you with an honor guard at the helicopter because, as you will soon realize, we didn't want to attract attention to this meeting."

Then CLIMBER said, "Take seats, gentlemen." He held in his hand for all to see an electronic remote control unit. Then he stepped to the platform, pressed a button and said, "I have just activated a special electronic field which renders this room impervious to any known intrusion or eavesdropping device." As he spoke, a notice flashed on the screen behind him, stating a briefing security classification of top secret, "What we are to discuss here and now, I say to you in deadly earnest, is the closest held secret since the atomic bomb." Looking directly at the president, he said, "I say *closest* because only those in this room and the task team members are privy to the information we will reveal in this briefing."

The Commander-in-Chief looked briefly around the conference table and noticed the absence of officials he expected to be there--the chairman of the Senate Armed Services Committee, the secretary of defense, and the secretary of the army. Instead, only the chairman of the joint chiefs (CLIMBER), a vice admiral (WIZARD) and General Betancourt (MULEY) and I (SCOOP) were in attendance. This only intensified his interest as CLIMBER continued. "Mr. President, you have inherited a legacy from three previous presidents, the first of whom, beginning twenty years ago, developed a concept which has become an effective tool to thwart Soviet ambitions outside their borders. This concept was withheld from the last president, by direction of his predecessor, for reasons which you can appreciate as obvious, and now by means of this briefing, the baton is being passed to you. Used properly with courage, it can as in the past manage serious situations to the very doorstep of Russia herself to prevent them from becoming crises. The skill of this small, tightly-organized force is demonstrated by the fact the Soviets have yet to learn who they are up against if in fact they feel there *is* an unknown force deployed against them. In each situation using this force, Soviet failures have appeared to be accidents or just plain bad luck. We have a track record of thirty-one successes and only one failure. About twelve years ago a mission was aborted, and most of the Task Team was recalled safely. But three very brave men died, taking with them the secret of MOPS."

As he spoke, the top-secret title flashed on the screen which read, Military Operatives to Prevent Subversion--MOPS.

"Successful beyond our wildest hopes, MOPS has become the cheapest, most effective means of inhibiting Soviet aggression and combating global terrorism. We have indeed terrorized the terrorists. Let me emphasize, sir, that this is your tool and operates only at your discretion under mission-type orders. It cannot deploy except by your order. If you as president choose never to use MOPS, it will simply cease to exist, except on paper, which will go into deep freeze to be resurrected and presented as a recommendation to the next president. However, it would be a terrible waste to dismantle this small but magnificent group of highly dedicated professionals only to find at some point in your administration a dire need for their timely services.

"Utilizing the full resources of our government's information and intelligence agencies, a small group of forty-three people have succeeded in reducing the Soviet apparatus for conducting subversive operations to a second class effort by eliminating their most skilled operatives in the field, without their knowing how it was done nor by whom. The CIA knows nothing of the help they have received in the field. Because MOPS operatives never permit themselves to come under surveillance, their pinpoint actions of short duration keep the enemy second-guessing themselves, and the organization has remained undetected by friend and foe alike."

During the hours that followed, the president was held spellbound by the narrative of successful missions and situations which called for the use of MOPS. Finally, CLIMBER closed the briefing by announcing, "Mr. President, if you wish, you and I can secretly tour the home of MOPS, code named MAGNOLIA, at your convenience. However, you are now sitting in the only MOPS facility outside MAGNOLIA. Obviously as the safe house of safe houses, MANOLIA is not a showplace. Outside of the tenants, the only people who have seen it are in this room. This briefing room is convenient to all and, hidden away in General Betancourt's office it is not likely to be compromised. Meetings of a policy nature will be held here."

The president was impressed with how much had been accomplished by so few. As it happened, an important plank in his party's platform was the streamlining of government bureaucracy. He had long held the view that fewer people, who were held accountable could accomplish more at less cost and would speed up the slowly turning wheels of government. Moreover, he felt the government of the people, by the people, and for the people had over time become the government of the politicians, by the politician, and for the politicians, serving themselves with little service to the nation. He was satisfied the era of the professional politician was over. As the briefing ended, he assured all present that under his administration, MOPS would be reactivated and continue to function as organized and further commented that next to squaring off in a personal duel with the chairman of the communist party, this sounded like the best way to fight a war, keeping thousands or even millions of innocent lives out of it.

As a patriot and an historian I am proud to say that the tattered American Flag shown anew and waved proudly over a nation reborn under God. Now it remained for a generation to be born again. So a new era, a new beginning in our nation's history had begun with the teaching of fundamental Christian principles, the very basis of the classroom. MOPS would be, though inconspicuous, a major player in the hidden field of clandestine foreign affairs. The people felt in charge and that the great lessons learned in our recovery must be remembered by future generations. Historians, including myself, were busy insuring that these lessons were not forgotten by recording accurately the saving events for posterity. It was also generally felt that we had earned God's blessing.

CHAPTER 6

ROAD BACK TO GREATNESS

WILLIAM TELL was happy to see that his alter ego Major Hunter William Bowman had just made the promotion list to Lieutenant Colonel; however, this did not mean a job change. We was still commander of task team WILLIAM TELL. As he studied areas of the world in which deployment was likely, he perceived a new respect for the United States. The world had witnessed democracy in action, a nonviolent retaking of power by the people without creating the necessary chaos, which invited foreign attempts at subversion. The people had corrected longtime misuse and abuse of power, setting once again a fine example to the world. The bright torch of liberty once again illuminated the road to peace.

Still there was the ever-present envy and hatred that had been directed at us for decades by envious and power-hungry despots of the world. Now they employed a new tactic—radicalizing the Muslim religion to cover a raw power grab. These were now the enemy, and the war rages on. It was imperative that we continued to support our God-ordained ally Israel, whom their enemies have vowed to destroy, as she continues to exist against all odds.

With the moratorium's end and acceptance of MOPS by the new president, CLIMBER decided to assemble all four ten-man task teams to bring them up to date. He would give them a pep talk and inform them of a change the president felt was necessary. He began the briefing,

"EVEREST is concerned that for several years since the birth of MOPS we have used the same code names. Granted, the frequency and short duration of deployment of any one task team makes compromise unlikely, but not impossible. There is no reason to think code names have been compromised, but it is good practice to change codes periodically. Also the president has directed we strike the word *military* from the title. Therefore, MOPS will become CSE—Counter Subversion Executive. The mission and organization remains unchanged. Only the code names will change to thicken the wall of secrecy. Hitherto, code names of operations were impersonal--OPERATION CROSSBOW and individuals were assigned personal code names--WILLIAM TELL. Hereafter designations will have no relationship to their use. This change applies only to the organization title and to the task team commanders. Effective immediately, these are the changes: MERLIN becomes HAMMER (HR). SIDEKICK becomes TORNADO (TR). VICEROY becomes MUSTANG (MG). WILLIAM TELL becomes SPIRIT (ST).

"You will note it is intentional that these new code names have no relationship with one another or to you as individuals. Numbered agents will add a letter pre-fix to their number. The letter will be the first letter of their team code number. S42 would be a member of Task Team SPIRIT. Memorize the new code names and mentally erase the old code names by using the new ones in conversations with each other, beginning immediately, when we are all here at MAGNOLIA.

"In addition, we will place additional emphasis on mission debriefing so as to provide EVEREST with as much intelligence as possible. Therefore, spying has become a legitimate sideline in that we gain much information during our missions. This means that through the president we will serve as a secret adjunct to our established intelligence community—more or less an extra duty. But, unlike the dirty game of espionage, CSE must continue to be unknown to friends and enemies alike by maintaining our lightning-strike style of operations. We are unique. Keep it that way. Don't let spying interfere with our primary mission to *plan carefully, strike boldly, and retire swiftly.*

"You are professionals and know the grim reality of a personal war, matching your wits with the enemy. In this kind of engagement you have four distinct advantages--the secrecy of your organization, you blend in since you wear no uniform, the brevity of your mission, and the element of surprise

"That's not to say there is little risk. Your wits and imagination are aided by careful planning and research prior to deployment. Train to hone your skills to a sharp edge and, like HAMMER, have an alternate plan for every situation—just in case. One might say we keep a low profile: I would rather it to be no profile. In other words, the term *low profile* would indicate the enemy knows something about us but very little. We must keep the enemy completely ignorant of CSE; not even a suspicion. The secrecy, nature and style of our work requires us to remain small—no empire building. In any organization there is always some ambitious one who wants to leave his mark by reinventing the wheel. Don't even think about it. We are not about to argue with our phenomenal success.

"Gentlemen, now it remains that we study and prepare ourselves for a mission directive from EVEREST which could come anytime."

* * *

Meanwhile, buried deep in the CIA, COUGAR was distressed at the news her boss and lover was dead. KRAIT had been her mentor and expressed his intention to promote her to Chief of Department V (V for violence) of the KGB, the dirty work department. It wasn't so much his death she regretted as it was the opportunity for promotion. She recalled her rape as a child by her father. In her young mind it was an ugly incident often repeated, against her will. Later, her damaged sexuality became a weapon to get what she wanted out of men ... and sometimes their lives. As an assassin she was proficient but never suspected. She had learned well from KRAIT. Her infiltration of the CIA had gone easier than expected. She had bedded with a member who eventually promised her a job in the organization. She pretended an intimate loving relationship to gain his confidence. On his recommendation and a cover story backed by cleverly forged documentation she was assigned a position at the European Desk—perfect. Frequent trips and assignment to Europe now made it easy to keep in touch with the KGB. She had heard from another agent that she was being sought by Kirishnin. She had been working under the control of Krait, but since his death she had been a mole in the CIA. Now it was time to reconnect.

The "Iron Duchess," Katrina Romanov, reported to KGB headquarters and was ushered to the office of Anatoly Kirishnin who asked sternly, "Where have you been?"

"I'm currently a mole in the CIA. KRAIT was my control. He wisely decided to keep my assignment secret until I was firmly ensconced and knew my capabilities in my new position. He said we would only meet at his direction. I was to check our message drop once a week, but I never heard from him. Then I discovered why. His death left me without control, and then I heard you were looking for me."

"Yes, I have broken into KRAIT's secret file and found your dossier. He thought very highly of you."

"He told me he would recommend my appointment as Chief of Department V."

"That may be, but I must weigh the advantages of the two positions before I make move. Will your position in the CIA contribute more to our mission? I've always thought an effective agent in the field is more beneficial than some desk job here, but as head of Department V, you will get your hands dirty, so to speak. Do you understand the mission of Department V?"

"Yes, sabotage, assassination and subversion-- in general, terrorism."

"And you can handle that?"

"Of course, personally if necessary. I don't see it as entirely a desk job."

Meanwhile, the CIA succeeded in eliminating several lines of investigation. They narrowed it down to two people, a man and a woman. The man in Washington was arrested, and the woman was determined to work for the European Desk. But she couldn't be located. A warrant for her arrest and her ID photo was issued to all CIA offices at home and abroad. Normally infiltrating a U.S. government agency was a lifetime assignment negating an agent's usefulness elsewhere because an ID photo and detailed information became a matter of record, real and bogus. Still bits and pieces of information gathered by Soviet agents outside the CIA warned that something hot was going on inside the agency. When this information was received in Moscow, COUGAR knew her cover had been blown because her American benefactor had been arrested. This information made the decision easy. COUGAR was now Chief of Department V. Kirishnin told an associate "I pity those who would oppose her."

COUGAR was as realistic as she was immoral. She knew there would be certain situations when a man would be more appropriate and effective than a woman. She began her search for a comrade in mischief--first a man who shared her vision for the job and second a trusted bed partner who would understand her need to bed with others in order to accomplish the mission. It didn't take long to find her man, another predator code-named

JACKAL. Naturally cougars and jackals don't get along well; but with COUGAR in a permanent state of heat, that antipathy was overcome and the two became a potent professional partnership in evil.

CHAPTER 7

WOLF IN SHEEP'S CLOTHING

The march of communism had slowed to a stroll. Vigilance was the by-word around the free world, yet the Soviets persisted with tactics designed to keep them in the shadows. By offering assistance to local revolutions, they helped create the chaos whereby the leaders can seize power. Continued assistance created an alliance the soviets could use to their advantage. The old tactic of hiding behind front organizations with names sounding patriotic to the locals was being applied to nations once again as it had been to Cuba, resulting in one dictator being replaced by another power-hungry despot. Americans finally understood and applied to world affairs the adage of looking beneath the sheep's clothing to find the wolf.

At home the general feeling was that the enemy within was under control and a return to prosperity required discipline and some belt tightening to stay the course outlined by the new president. We had a plan, and we were confident it was the open road to moral and economic recovery—in that order. The president reminded us of the words of Benjamin Franklin,

> "God governs in the affairs of man. And if a sparrow cannot fall to the ground without His notice, is it probable that an empire can rise without His aid? We have been assured in the Sacred Writings that except the Lord build the house, they labor in vain that build it. I firmly believe that, without His concurring aid, we shall succeed in this political building no better that the builders of Babel."

Yes, God is in control and he will not bless a sinful nation. In contrast, the world's power mongers never give up until they are totally destroyed. The president subscribed to the old adage, *the best defense is a strong offense.* Defense hands the initiative to the enemy. Offense keeps him off-balance and wondering where he'll be hit next. It is up to us to keep the pressure on. The president was grateful for the gift he was given. CSE was just the tool to keep the pressure on without wholesale bloodshed. Simply put, he would tell CSE what to do, a mission, and let them concoct a plan for how best to do it. He understood CSE functions best early in the game when the threat is still manageable, giving the task teams the most options.

The president mulled over his options. Intelligence summaries painted a dark picture. To the ill-informed the threat seemed to demand deadly force, armed intervention to salvage American interests in the region. But this president as a matter of policy intended to avoid commitment of the military as long as he had a viable option. In this case we were facing the threat of radical Islam, a splinter group using religious beliefs to recruit suicide bombers to attack Christian nations. America had felt the impact with attacks on the World Trade Center and the burning of our forests.

Assembled in the situation room of the White House the president's advisors were at a loss as to how to handle a request for assistance from the Prime Minister of Australia. During the PM's visit to the United States, long discussions about the problem ended with assurances of cooperation. Without compromising CSE, the president hinted that he had success in this area of subversion and if he could offer secret help he'd do so. He was especially impressed with the PM's public statement to his people on the subject. I have substituted in his statement two references; *World Trade Center* and *Americans*--to bring this statement home to our people. Otherwise his statement is quoted verbatim. Reflecting his firm resolve, here is what he said,

> "Immigrants, not Americans, must adapt. Take it or leave it. I am tired of this nation worrying about whether we are offending some individual or culture. Since the terrorist attack on the World Trade Center, we have experienced a surge in patriotism by the majority of Americans. This culture has been developed over three centuries of struggle, trials and victories, by millions of men and women who have sought freedom.
> We speak English, not Spanish, Lebanese, Arabic, Chinese, Russian, or any other language. Therefore, if you wish to become part of our society, learn the language!
>
> Most Americans believe in God. This is not some Christian, right wing, political push, but a fact, because Christian men and women, on Christian principles founded this nation, and this is clearly documented. It's certainly appropriate to display it on the walls of our schools. If God offends you, then I suggest another part of the world as your new home, because God is part of our culture. We will accept your beliefs, and not question why. All

we ask is that you accept ours, and live in harmony and peaceful enjoyment with us.

This is our country, our land, and our lifestyle, and we will allow you every opportunity to enjoy all of this. But once you are done complaining, whining, and griping about Our Flag, Our Pledge, Our Christian beliefs, or our Way of Life, I highly encourage you to take advantage of another great American freedom, *the right to leave.*

If you aren't happy here then leave. We didn't force you to come here. You asked to be here. So accept the country *you* accepted."

The president felt that this was a courageous man and a staunch ally he'd like to help, and if assistance could be at little cost, so much the better. The removal of radical Muslim leaders in country must appear to be accidental or the work of an unknown third party so as to give the PM "plausible deniability." Based on past experience, CSE could guarantee that to be the case. The president looked around the situation room table, caught the eye of the chairman of the joint chiefs of staff, and doodled on the pad before him the secret circle X signal. The chairman nodded that he understood he was to return to the president one hour after the adjournment of the meeting.

An hour later the chairman sat before the president in the privacy of the Oval Office.

"CLIMBER, I need your advice. Is counter subversion assistance to Australia a viable option at this time? This would be my first CSE mission directive, and frankly I want to be reasonably sure of success."

"In this case Mr. President, we have little intelligence to go on, being Australia is an ally. What is the nature of the threat on the ground? What has the PM told you?"

"As you know, all nations professing to be Christian are potential targets for Muslin extremists, and Australia is no exception. They have been seriously attacked by terrorists. The PM wants to make it so hot for them that they will see the futility in attacking a free Christian Australia. He set the tone of their resistance in his public statements. However, reports from the aborigines in the isolated areas of the Northern Territories and Western Australia indicate a terrorist training camp may have been established."

"Then why doesn't he use his armed forces to clear them out?"

"Because he would like them to think they are fighting moderate Muslims who've made Australia their home. A citizen uprising, which would conduct a successful strike implicating the moderate Muslims, might encourage them to take sides, one way or another. In that way the government might identify friend from foe and deport the extremist."

"I have high confidence CSE can handle the job, Mr. President, given time to prepare."

"How long?"

"We'll begin our studies on the area immediately. We need satellite photos of the region to familiarize my people with the topography and vegetation. It would be desirable if the aborigines could pinpoint the camp within a radius of five miles. To be fair to our teams we could use two weeks since we're starting cold."

"OK CLIMBER, I'll see what the CIA has and speak to the PM."

"Thank you sir, we'll begin with a study of the aboriginal culture, so if need be, they can be approached without offense. MAGNOLIA has one of the finest political science libraries in the country, but I'm not sure we have all we'll need about the native population. If we can find an expert, it would be helpful. We can set up a class away from MAGNOLIA to protect our security."

"Alright, I'll check with the PM; you guys are thorough. aren't you?"

"Over the years we have learned that we never know what small piece of information can spell the difference between success and failure."

"I suppose that covers it for now, CLIMBER. I'll hold the mission directive until I have more. Meantime, get started with your studies."

"Wilco (will comply). Thank you, sir. CSE will do all we can to make your first use of us a success.

The call came over MAGNOLIA's intercom to assemble in the briefing room. Two teams bored and itching for action were available. WIZARD mounted the platform. Emblazoned on the rostrum was the motto of CSE: *Plan Carefully, Strike Boldly, Retire Swiftly*

"Okay, settle down." Pointing to the motto he said, "When the Commandos came up with that motto, they didn't have CSE in mind, but I can't see a better fit. We have good reason to believe a study of Australia is appropriate and a mission directive may be imminent. I can't be specific yet, but we will live up to the first item of our motto, *plan carefully*. I know Australia is a big country, but I recommend you focus on topography of the various regions, especially isolated northern regions. We'll be specific if and when we receive EVEREST's mission directive. Okay, go to work.

* * *

COUGAR and JACKAL lay in bed. After a lustful episode they began to discuss the next step in their support of Muslim terrorists in Australia. COUGAR asked, "Did you arrange for delivery of plastic explosives to Ahmud's group?"

JACKAL replied, "Yes, it's all set. I'm going myself. A submarine is due to land me and the boxes at a prearranged isolated site on the north east coast of the Western Australia near his camp. I visited him two weeks ago at his camp on Java and gave him twelve AK-47s, and plenty of ammunition. The hidden site he has selected in Western Australia will be useful for some time to come. With these supplies, they should be able to do a lot of damage for such a small force. Half his force are suicidal religious fanatics who will gladly die for their cause in exchange for the promise of delights to come."

"I just don't understand how they can talk them into such foolishness, but as long as it helps our cause we can use them."

"They can certainly create the chaos we need to start our brand of subversion."

"When can we expect them to start moving?"

"Ahmud said he needed at least two weeks to finish their training. Then he expects to send bombers to Perth, Adelaide, Sidney and Melbourne. His tactic is to create a diversion to draw police away from the intended target. The targets will be hit simultaneously, so the populace will have no doubt it was a terrorist strike.."

"Da, that will be a good start."

CHAPTER 8

CODE NAME: SPIRIT

"Bill darling?" called Toni.
"Yes, love."

"If I'd known moving to my office here in Atlanta would double my business, I'd have been here long ago. This close to my markets has turned out to be a real advantage. New clients are now coming to me."

"As for me, Tierra Blanca was a long commute. I don't know about your new clients, but I'd come to your office just to get a look at such a lovely creature."

"Flatterer."

"Oh no, flattery is telling someone they are something they're not or an exaggeration. In my book you cannot be flattered. Your beauty goes far beyond the limits of exaggeration."

"Where do you come up with all that stuff?"

"As the old song goes my love, *you are my inspiration.*"

"Just hold that thought."

"You've done wonders with this condo. It's palatial compared to my old digs."

"Thank you my dear, but I dread that red light buzzer."

"I know, but at least it shouldn't be a lengthy absence."

"Thankfully."

Toni, the educated chef, had planned a sumptuous meal. Bill had become used to her delectable offerings, but he never failed to show his appreciation. She glowed in his adoration. Bill showed his love in every way, and she never doubted it. She felt secure and sheltered in his love. Although secret to the world, between themselves their marriage was open and intimate and true to their marriage vows. They both felt God's blessing. They were grateful for the two weeks of marital bliss they shared. Then, one late night the red light and buzzer intruded into their heaven.

Bill acknowledged the call using a pay phone miles away and then reported to MAGNOLIA in time for a full briefing on the mission directive from EVEREST. Having been fully briefed by CLIMBER, WIZARD took the rostrum and began, "Well, it's been a while, and for the first time we will begin a mission with a new name, Counter Subversion Executive, CSE. Idle for so long it is up to me to pick the Task Team for the first mission, and I will in a moment. The nature of the mission may require more than one team or possibly a reinforced team, so listen carefully.

"We've had you on a study of Australia based on a hunch, that hunch proved correct. EVEREST has had long talks with the Prime Minister of Australia and, without revealing our identity, offered help with a serious problem. Aborigines have reported what appears to be a terrorist training camp in an isolated area near the rugged north coast of Western Australia about 400 miles southwest of Darwin as the crow flies. It looks like our mission will take a Commando-style raid designed to leave no survivors and take no prisoners. We believe the terrorists are supported by Department V of the KGB. The camp must be destroyed leaving evidence that the raid was participated in by moderate Muslims living in Australia. Later I'll take your ideas about how we can constitute such evidence. The PM wants to smooth over the relationship between citizens and moderate Muslims who have chosen to live in the country, and perhaps recruit some of them to infiltrate terrorist organizations in country.

"The area of operations being unfamiliar and the enemy strength being uncertain we'll start by deploying a ten man team to assess the situation on the ground and formulate a plan of attack. SPIRIT, you're it."

"Aye, sir."

"You will embark twenty men on an aircraft carrier at Alameda, whose mission will take them through the East Indies, and rendezvous with a submarine at sea. There you'll board the sub with ten men. If your assessment on the ground requires more men, they can be dropped at a drop zone you designate. The sub will insert you at a designated point west of Darwin and lie submerged in wait 'til you finish your mission. They will relay any radio message you need to send. Otherwise, you will maintain radio silence. Additional men from the carrier, if needed, will be dropped free fall at night. We don't want to attract attention with helicopters or low flying aircraft in the area. Our operation will require stealth and sudden violence, so the mission is hereby designated SILENT THUNDER. SPIRIT, if there is anything you need we will notify our service facilitators with our usual K2 priority. If you have any ideas, clear them with me before you leave. Once you do leave the whole show is up to you. The only Australian to know about this action is the PM, and he will have no clear idea where or exactly when. He has issued an order to the armed forces to stay clear of the area for the next thirty days. This is our chance to prevent serious damage to a faithful ally without their knowing it and without glory. Someday our story will be told; let's make this a glowing chapter."

WIZARD then turned the briefing over to SPIRIT, "The first thing that strikes me is fall here is spring in Australia. The mission directive as described by WIZARD causes me to envision a night combat action timed to take advantage of moonlight. We'll carry light packs with dry rations for five days and black clothing that will not reveal our identity. In the event that the terrain dictates a change of clothing we'll carry alternate covering. We will carry a basic load of ammunition. The weapons and ammunition will be of foreign manufacture so that spent cartridges when found will not implicate the United States. Special footwear will leave no tracks that can be traced to us. There may be a need for plastic explosives in this operation to create a diversion and to destroy explosives and weapons stored at the site. I'll need two demolition specialist and everyone else cross-trained. I see an ambush raid on the camp, quick and violent, leaving no one alive to tell the tale. I don't know how long it will take to locate the camp, so study the satellite photos for likely spots, probably hidden below the horizon in desolate country or beneath trees where they exist. Another thing just occurred to me. Down-Under, there exists wild life found nowhere else in the world as well as snakes and crocodiles. Since some of the north coast of Australia consists of mangrove swamps, we're sure to encounter some of these early, so you two paramedics should be prepared with antitoxin. Remember this--do not discard ration wrappers; keep all trash in your packs. We don't want to leave behind any sign we were there. Until we know more, that's all I have for now. When we depart depends on the moon phase and the navy. If any of you have questions come and see me. Once again, you will carry no identification. That's all, Go to work."

Three days later SPIRIT called a meeting of the twenty man team,

"Okay, men, we have the information we need to get moving. Here's the lay-out: the navy will fly us to Alameda, where we'll board the carrier and sail to the Coral Sea to rendezvous with the submarine. Due to the brevity of our mission, the carrier can linger in the area in case we need more men. Understand that some of you may merely be taking a long ocean voyage, but be ready. We don't know the conditions on the ground or the strength of the enemy. The PM has notified us that the aborigines have given us the approximate location of the camp within a five-mile radius. And wouldn't you know it, the location is just south of the longest stretch of mangrove swamp on the coast. That's good and bad--good because the enemy would not expect an attack from that direction and bad because we have to penetrate a critter infested swamp to reach the camp. Once inland, the trees are so sparse they can't be used for camouflage. That means we should look for a depression that can't be seen from a distance."

When SPIRIT finish, WIZARD asked him to report to his office. Arriving, he saw CLIMBER as well. Both wore beaming smiles prompting SPIRIT to ask, "What's so funny?"

"Not funny—pride." answered CLIMBER.

Thereupon SPIRIT was quietly promoted to Lieutenant Colonel with hardy congratulations. Surprised, SPIRIT said, "That was quick. The list was published only three weeks ago. I had a pretty high number. I looked forward to a six month wait."

"Well, they have their timetable and we have ours." said CLIMBER.

Then WIZARD added, "Start working on full Colonel and you might have my job when I retire."

SPIRIT smiled and added, "Speaking for the rest of us, we all hope that's a long way off, sir."

"That's one of your strengths. You always say the right thing."

"Like my daddy used to say, *Be truthful, and if you can't say something good about someone, keep your trap shut.*"

Later, SPIRIT returned to WIZARD with an idea. He knew that after the ambush whoever comes to that site will find total destruction with bodies left where they fell. They'll also find a few leaflets, calling cards from moderate Muslims decrying terrorism but making it plain they would fight with terrorism of their own if need be. It should convey the message to stay out of Australia. WIZARD thought for a moment and replied, "Good, TORNADO is a graduate of the Defense Language Institute in Arabic. He can help make it authentic. He can bang it off on his computer today because you haven't much time. I was just about to call you. The carrier leaves Alameda in three days. You leave tomorrow. Have your people draw their equipment and weapons immediately. Your C-130 departs Andrews Air Force Base at 1000 hours tomorrow. The next morning found Team SPIRIT airborne and on their way to Alameda Naval Air Station in California.

As a young teenager SPIRIT's dad's WWII service was aboard the fast carrier USS Yorktown CV10, aka. The Fighting Lady, as part of Task Force 58. During the war the boy had fished from the pier many times and his memories seemed more vivid than ever at the sight of the huge nuclear powered USS Enterprise. Leading his twenty man team up the gangway he paused at the top, turned, and saluted the ensign then saluted the officer of the deck and asked, "Permission to come aboard, Sir."

"Permission granted."

The captain, who was standing nearby, came to SPIRIT, extended his hand and said, "Welcome aboard the 'Big E.' We've been expecting you." He turned to a sailor he said, "Show these men to their quarters." Then he turned back to SPIRIT. "He will be your guide for the first three days until you know your way around. This ship can be a real puzzle to a landlubber. We'll talk later in my quarters. I'll send for you."

"Aye-Aye, Sir.

CHAPTER 9

SILENT THUNDER

The nuclear powered Big E was fast and the Pacific Ocean vast. The task force commander was Rear Admiral Frederick Jackson who called Task Team SPIRIT together to explain that the ready room they were in would be theirs for the duration of the voyage. He further explained, "Constant air operations are vital for the protection of the task force. In no way is this to be a pleasure cruise. There will be many battle station drills during the voyage. In such a drill your battle station will be this ready room. Your authority for being here is the chairman of the joint chiefs—that's all we need to know. We are to rendezvous with the submarine USS Carp, a diesel boat. Yes, we still have a few in commission from which we can draw trained submariners for our nuclear attack subs. The sub will transport you to your designated point of insertion. It is the navy's business to know the waters of the world. In this case, you'll be happy to learn, the mangrove swamp is navigable by rubber rafts for three fourths of the way to dry terrain. The rest of the way you'll have to hack your way through undergrowth in knee-deep water. We estimate the swamp to be about a hundred yards deep. Stay clear of any grassy mounds. They probably protect crocodile eggs and mothers will be thereabout. For reinforcement in a hurry we have an aircraft onboard to fill that role, if needed. We were told no helicopters. That's about all we can help you with, whatever your mission."

"Thank you Sir."

At the departure of the Admiral SPIRIT continued, "Okay. With that useful information let's go to work on contingency plans to cover any situation we might encounter. Use your imagination. You four communicators have our call signs worked out with the carrier and the sub. All this may sound superfluous because you are all pros at this game, but we are dealing out death. We don't want death dealt to us." At this point S42 stood up and asked, "Sir, would you lead us in prayer?"

"Certainly..." SPIRIT bowed his head and prayed, "Almighty God, we are about to embark on a mission to take lives in the full knowledge that without Your sanction we would be committing murder. Just as you told the children of Israel to wipe out all the people of the land You promised and take possession of it because they were evil, we believe we are the instrument of Your will in this operation. We ask that You bless our arms in this endeavor and see us safely home. In Jesus' precious name we pray,

And everyone said, "Amen."

Upon arrival at the rendezvous a memorial ceremony was conducted for those who were lost in our first sea victory of WWII, the Battle of the Coral Sea. No sooner had the ceremony ended when the USS Carp surfaced a short distance away. SPIRIT bid their hosts goodbye and the 10-man team was lowered in a whale boat with all their gear and transferred to the sub.

SPIRIT could hardly believe his eyes, the skipper was Commander Trigertha, who helped his team exit Tierra Blanca during OPERATION ARROW.

"Ahoy, Trigger! This is a small world. Remember me?"

"Do I! You never let me win at cribbage."

"I see you got your third stripe. Congratulations."

"Yes, this is my last mission on a diesel. I'm taking command of a nuke when I get home. The navy finally recognized my genius, but don't tell them I can't win at cribbage."

"That's my secret. I may need a favor from you someday. This is bigger than your last boat."

"Yes, she's designed to carry troops on missions like yours. You'll find plenty of room to stow your gear. As soon as you're settled we'll work out the details of your mission."

With gear stowed and the comfort of his men seen to SPIRIT met with "Trigger" in the officer's ward room.

"We were in port on Guam when I received sealed orders to rendezvous with the Enterprise in the Coral Sea. It said I was to take on 10 passengers and drop you somewhere on the north coast of Australia."

A detailed chart of the northern Australian coastline was spread on the table, and SPIRIT picked up the calipers and drew circle and said, "Somewhere within that circle is our target." Then he pointed to the most desirable place at which his team could be inserted and asked Commander Trigertha, "Do you know of any reason to change the point?"

Trigger checked the depth of Timor Sea close to the point and agreed, "The sea is deep enough to lie in wait submerged. It is within sight of land, so signal lights can be used. Paddling distance will be reasonable for your men."

They agreed to maintain radio silence for three days. At the end of that time, silence would be broken to explain the delay--the call to be initiated by SPIRIT. In the meantime the sub would surface each morning at 0130 hours and wait 30 minutes for SPIRIT's signal before submerging. The same technique used to retrieve the team at Tierra Blanca will be used. Upon completion of the mission the sub would disembark the team at Sidney where the PM had booked a diplomatic courier flight back to Washington.

Next it was up to SPIRIT to locate the camp site, assess the situation on the ground and formulate the ambush plan.

The uncertain situation would test the imagination and audacity which had become almost second nature to the men of CSE.

The "S-Men," as SPIRIT's men had taken to calling themselves, prepared their gear and weapons for action. By now all were veterans of this type of warfare and confident in the outcome. So there was laughing and joking as they worked and exercised during the three-night cruise. They were impressed with the quality of food on board and enjoyed the movies, particularly since there were no war movies. Trigger said on each cruise he showed all twenty-six episodes of "Victory at Sea" so sailors can appreciate their proud history, all of which had been shown prior to team SPIRIT's arrival. The Carp was long out of Pearl and due back at the end of this mission.

The Carp arrived in daylight, and while submerged, they scanned the area for intruders. As expected, the region was deserted. A periscope search revealed a good point of entry to the mangrove swamp. After locating a suitable spot, the Carp stayed submerged until two hours before dawn to allow the team to enter the swamp in darkness and to exit in daylight to survey the lay of the land. Moonlight was at three-quarter phase—perfect.

The Carp broke the surface quietly through a light chop--no problem for five-man rubber rafts to negotiate. The team would use two rafts and tow an empty third just in case. As the team came on deck Trigger turned to SPIRIT and said, "Keep your head down shipmate. I'd hate to lose a good cribbage player."

"Let's remember this is a round trip, so don't go away."

Rafts loaded, the team began stroking the quarter mile toward the tangled shore. The Admiral was right. The frogmen who help chart this shore had done a good job. His information was accurate. The tough part was hacking their way through tangled brush in knee-deep swamp. All appreciated S24's foresight in including hip boots in their gear, not that we minded getting our feet wet. It served as protection against snakebites, which as it turned out was needed. We saw no other evidence of anyone else's attempts to hack their way through. One five-foot crocodile showed no curiosity and swam by, apparently not hungry. Everyone was glad they had taken the time to hone their machetes to a sharp edge. A short way from the swamp exit, they found an ideal spot to hide their rafts. Then very carefully the team moved to the nearest high ground about twenty-one feet above sea level to search the area with powerful field glasses. Searching 180 degrees, there was nothing but arid country, not sandy but not much vegetation to obstruct their view.

* * *

With no human being within thirty miles of their camp, JACKAL felt as secure as the terrorist. He arrived at the camp to create good will by providing weapons and explosives to assist their effort. He was treated like a welcome guest. Secure or not, they had taken the precaution of locating the camp in a depression similar to a shallow box canyon so as not to be seen from a distance as SPIRIT expected they would. Therefore, it would take some searching to find them. JACKAL was informed they had set the date for their simultaneous attacks on the four cities ten days hence. Then they were careless. To celebrate the arrival of the wherewithal to do their mischief, they built a campfire. SPIRIT could only think that providential as God's gift to his team, who spotted the smoke just before dark. There would be no sleep this night for the team.

Ahmud felt they were too isolated to need sentries, and JACKAL agreed. SPIRIT and S24 left the rest of the team and carefully advanced toward the camp to scout the situation, expecting to locate sentry positions. Pleasantly surprised, there were none. They crawled to the rim, careful not to silhouette themselves against the moon. SPIRIT counted twenty-five men, four of whom were Russian, at or near the fire. He couldn't help comparing the camp to a frying pan with the handle the only way out—a perfect killing ground. They would never have a better chance to do what they came to do. SPIRIT and S24 returned to the team to lay out the plan,

"Here's the situation. There were no sentries. We were able to get a clear view of the camp. We counted twenty-five men in the camp. Between the firelight and the moonlight, we have clear targets. Here's how we'll set up. The camp is situated in a frying pan layout with the handle the only way out. We'll split up into five two-man teams. With the handle at twelve o'clock, S18 and S21, your field of fire will be from twelve to three o'clock. S27 and S30, your field of fire will be from three o'clock to six o'clock. S13 and S17 from six o'clock to nine o'clock, and S16 and S15 from nine o'clock to twelve o'clock. S24 and I will cover the escape route, the handle. We'll take up an L position to achieve a cross fire. When your assigned killing zone is cleared, shift your fire to help the others. Take ten minutes to get into position on the rim opposite the handle. S15 has the farther to go so wait for him to fire the first shot. Then open up on them. Time check. Set your watches. The time is 2121 hours—now. After the ambush we must go into the camp to be certain every man is dead and scatter the leaflets. Any questions? No? Move out!"

Within twenty seconds of the first shot, the withering fire had done its job. It was a testament to the marksmanship and professional efficiency of CSE. Still, in a situation like this, wounded might recover, so it was necessary to enter the camp to administer the *coup de grace*. Each two-man team went to their assigned quarter and fired one shot into the head each body as they lay. JACKAL, hit twice, lay wounded, and just before the fatal bullet, he spit upon his executioner. Then, the demolitionists prepared the charges to set off all the explosives and destroy the weapons JACKAL brought with him. Once clear of the camp, they detonated the charges electronically. The powerful blast sent a shock wave that was felt by the team, and the explosion, heard many miles away, lit the night sky so that even at a great distance it could have been seen. Their job done the team paused momentarily to give thanks to God for His part in the ease of their mission.

But as if he had heard a voice from within, SPIRIT had second thoughts. With the camp destroyed in spectacular fashion, it occurred to him that if there were others nearby, they'd surely investigate. It would have been easy to leave the scene and call the mission successful, but playing his hunch, he led his team to a spot where they could keep the destroyed camp under surveillance for 24 hours. They didn't need that long. Just after daylight they observed four armed men arriving from southwesterly direction. SPIRIT watched as they searched the area and reasoned the men couldn't have come far and probably waited until daylight to investigate the explosion. He saw the possibility of another campsite nearby. Calling his team together to explain his estimate of the situation, he asked. "What's our ammo situation?"

S24 responded, "The ambush was so brief we used only a quarter of our ammo."

"Good, here's what we'll do. I'll take S15 with me and trail the four back to where they came from. S24, you take charge here and follow at a distance, careful not to lose sight of us and careful not to expose yourselves. I would estimate we should see their destination within three hours at the most. If after that time we see nothing, we'll consider our mission accomplished, but if we find their camp, we'll work out a plan to finish our mission. It appears from their body language that the four men were familiar with the campsite and concluded its destruction was Allah's will because they knelt toward Mecca and prayed." SPIRIT turned and crawled to the crest of a mound and through his field glasses observed their departure. SPIRIT looked at S15 and said, "Okay, let's go."

They reached the small camp in only an hour. Having observed the situation they backtracked to the rest of the team. SPIRIT explained, "Judging from the size of their camp and the fact that it is situated near what appears to be a well-worn road, I'd say they were there to give warning to the main camp. There are only ten men, and there is no question that they are Muslim and armed. Again, we saw no sentries. This appears to be a situation of overkill. With their main camp destroyed I expect them to pack up and leave by the way they came, so we have to hit them now in daylight. Fortunately, we can approach their camp unseen to within small arms range. Then we'll form a line of skirmishers. OK, count off!"

Each member of the team uttered a number one through ten..

"There are 10 targets. Each of us will fire from the prone position at our counterpart from left to right. If you are as good as I think you are, one volley will do the job instantly. Then we'll move in to be sure of our work."

The plan was perfect but the execution was not. One target was missed and began to run for cover, but was promptly taken under fire by all 10 of the team. Amazingly he was rigged to be a suicide bomber and blew up when hit. He was prepared to die if discovered and arrested and take his captors with him. Team SPIRIT moved in and found all were dead but finished the job nevertheless.

Returning, the team moved quickly to their rubber rafts and into the swamp to be ready for the second 0130 surface of the *Carp*. During their wait at 2200 hours an Australian Coast Guard patrol boat cruised by but showed no sign of sighting the team. The *Carp* surfaced on time. SPIRIT signaled the sub which had surfaced with deck awash so the team could paddle aboard. As the rafts approached, Trigger called out, "Successful mission?"

To which SPIRIT replied, "Yes, God was with us."

Trigger then looked down the hatch and ordered, "Send the success message."

The rafts quickly deflated and stowed, the team went below. It was difficult not to share their success with the crew, but the S-Men kept silent about their thunder. One crewman was heard to say, "What's the matter with these guys, they should be celebrating."

The Enterprise, scheduled to show the flag at Sidney, dropped the other ten men to join SPIRIT and his team at the airbase to return home. All were dressed in casual clothes and boarded the air force diplomatic courier flight to the U.S.

CLIMBER received the message from the Carp that the mission was a complete success and passed the information to EVEREST, who notified the Prime Minister. On arrival at MAGNOLIA the team was debriefed. SPIRIT made it his business to give credit to the most important member of his team—God. The team was reminded of the many times in the Bible where God struck terror into the enemy enabling the Israelites to destroy a far superior force.

* * *

JACKAL had been tight-lipped about his part in the plan to strike terror in the four Australian cities. He was prepared to claim he had set it up had it been a success. So when COUGAR had not heard from him for an unusually long period, she didn't know what to think. Also there has been no indication of recent terrorist activity in Australia. Because of the location and the nature of the CSE operation, it could be years before it would be clear what happened to JACKAL—if ever. The Iron Duchess was left to wonder.

* * *

The president was impressed with the economy and the results of OPERATION SILENT THUNDER. The navy didn't need to stray far from their primary mission to provide the needed assistance. With this experience behind him he felt comfortable with his new tool and better understood the successes of previous presidents.

Because of the long voyage the mission took longer than usual, and Bill was headed for a homecoming he'd never forget, his first since his marriage. He arrived at the Atlanta condo midday while Toni was at work, so he showered and fixed himself lunch. He decided not to call her. She'd be home soon. And it wasn't long before he heard the key in the door. Toni entered, loaded with groceries, not noticing Bill standing in the living room. As she headed for the kitchen, she saw Bill, screamed, dropped the groceries, and flew into his arms, locking her legs around him as he stood and kissed him long and wet. She felt so good in his arms as she whispered, "Take me to bed, my love."

With homecomings like this he almost wished for more frequent missions, but on second thought the intervals were also blissful.

CHAPTER 10

GENTLEMEN AVENGERS

Team SPIRIT routinely assembled for their debriefing. OPERATION SILENT THUNDER was an inexpensive counter move against a vicious wantonly savage enemy who made it necessary for good and decent men to become assassins. The only thing this enemy understands is the terrorism they force on us returned in kind--vicious and without quarter. SPIRIT seemed disturbed about something, so after the debriefing he called the twenty men together. "Gentlemen, and that's exactly what you are, gentlemen forced by circumstances to become avengers in the defense of our homeland. Fighting this evil takes us all over the world to keep this enemy from our shores. We are not fighting uniformed armies. Instead we are fighting a personal battle against animals out to kill us if they can. We are uniquely organized to fight such a battle. We are doing the dirty work we are designed to do, and that takes a special breed of soldier. We few, in the long run, are saving thousands, maybe millions of lives while taking a few. The lives saved owe us a debt they cannot pay and if they could, we cannot accept. Why am I repeating something you already know?

"During the ambush you all did your job well, but when we entered the camp to finish what we came to do, I noticed some of your faces. It was apparent that standing over a wounded man and shooting him where he lay was repugnant to some of you. And that only shows you to be civilized men. I know the feeling you must have felt, but you must understand that if any of the enemy had survived to tell the story, the price we would have to pay later would be much higher. Case in point, we are still paying the price for the disobedience of Joshua and the children of Israel when entering the Promised Land. God told Joshua to kill every man, woman, and child and take possession of the land. He even set the boundaries of the land. Those boundaries were never achieved because as kind hearted people they made deals with their enemies and even intermarried with them. Since then the Promised Land has endured conflicting religions and nations in a constant state of war. Israel has never known real peace. Today we are fighting that same war, and since 1948, Israel has survived against all odds. So you see, we must finish each mission we are given so it will not come back and bite us.

"As a young Lieutenant in the Korean War, I learned that lesson well. When you see the enemy not as people, but as demons bent on destroying you, then your job-well-done will be a source of satisfaction and a quiet pride in accomplishment. When you leave the battle arena and return home, you will not carry with you a burden of guilt because God is with you when you do His will. In Judges Chapter 6:12, the angel of the lord appeared to Gideon and said, "The Lord is with you, O valiant warrior." Our way of life is God-given. Radical Muslims feel the same way, but there is a difference; Muhammad lies dead in his grave, but Jesus' tomb is empty. He rose from the dead and was seen by over five hundred eyewitnesses before ascending to sit at the right hand of God. Our Founding Fathers, following God's instruction, created the United States of America, and many have died defending it. We, you and I, have the privilege of defending the country we love."

The S-Men, their minds relieved, came to their feet and applauded SPIRIT's words. One by one they filed out of the briefing room, pausing to shake his hand. WIZARD had listened carefully to SPIRIT's message and stayed behind to talk with him.

"You have a gift, the knack of saying just what's needed when it's needed."

"Thank you sir, but I just said what I felt."

"That's just what I mean—a gift. If you hadn't said it, I would because during the debriefing I could see in the manner of a few of your men the need to clarify the necessity of the mission, just as you did."

SPIRIT replied, "I'm proud to serve with such men, but from time to time in this dirty business, men of great character and humanity need a reminder."

Thus ended OPERATION SILENT THUNDER. It now became number thirty-two in the list of successes credited to the Counter Subversion Executive. Being a former business man the president was so impressed with his new tool that he almost wanted to advertise for additional opportunities to employ CSE—a chilling thought to the security minded CLIMBER and WIZARD. Nevertheless the president authorized The Silver Star for all team personnel.

Routinely, the president was given an intelligence briefing once a week, but he became so interested in intelligence summaries he increased the frequency in order to detect situations requiring early response and the possible use of CSE. The move was to pay great dividends later in his administration.

* * *

In COUGAR's desire for answers she sent an agent to the campsite. The shallow box canyon had become a giant crater— all that remained of the terrorist training camp. However he found, a few feet outside the crater, a charred leaflet to answer her question. When told of the find she responded, "Well, that's that. For the present, Australia is too expensive." and turned her attention elsewhere.

Her ties to Muslim terrorists were still intact, and she let it be known she was ready and willing to assist in their fight. It wasn't long until she heard from radical Muslim cleric Saddam Amabo, known to have directed terrorist attacks in England, Spain and several other countries. Amabo's approach to Islam was in twisted error.

* * *

Allow me to interject this thought. Our understanding of Christianity must not be in error, to which so many well-meaning people, and even clergy, have fallen. Here is the essence of SPIRIT's last counseling session with his men:

"How do we relate God's Word to our mission? What gives us as a people the power to do what we must do—fight evil? Just as with the men of CSE, training alone is not the whole answer. First we must understand evil in order to recognize it. What is evil? Evil is that which opposes or contradicts the Holy Word of God. Yes, it's that simple, but many have discarded God's Word without ever studying it or understanding its love and protection. As the guide to a happy and contented life, it stands alone. Designed by a superior intelligence, there is no better way, and it must be understood that if we are to be "born again" into a new relationship with God, we must *know* Him. There is no limit to His power. If we are ignorant of His Word, we don't recognize His power when it is exercised. We often chalk it up as coincidence, not understanding that often coincidence is when God wishes to remain anonymous. Knowing we are on God's side and we are instruments of His will, the force of his power is with us. Prayer is not a now-and-then thing. Benjamin Franklin said, 'Work as if you'll live a hundred years. Pray as if you are to die tomorrow.' Every day is a living prayer. The Bible says we must pray without ceasing. We are in constant communication with Almighty God. This realization must be apparent to every citizen as it was to our Founding Fathers and is to the men of CSE."

Someone once asked, "Are we standing on principle or loitering on the perimeter?" This statement brings to mind the story of a mother who having just put her young son to bed, heard a thump. She rushed into his room to find he had fallen out of bed and lying on the floor. She said, "What happened?"

Her little boy replied, "I don't know. I guess I stayed too close to where I got in."

That's the way many people fall out of faith. They stay too close to where they got in. We need to stay close to our God by studying his word. A shallow faith is an invitation the Devil is eager to accept.

CHAPTER 11

CHAMELEON

At the evil end of the spectrum of good and evil, COUGAR's devious mind mulled over her next outrageous gambit-- where, when and how to strike at the free world. She felt inhibited somewhat by the fact that her stint in the CIA resulted in her picture being placed in the hands of the all the intelligence agencies of the free world. Nevertheless, without JACKAL, she felt it necessary to take personal charge in the field, but with a price on her head, so to speak, that would be risky.

Stepping out of the shower she stood before a mirror thinking, *That's the body that killed seventeen men. I can't change that nor would I want to, but the face and the hair can change. So easy for a woman.* She studied her head and face, her brown hair, her dark brown eyes, the shape of her mouth, and her eyebrows. She thought, *Change all these, and I could be a different woman, free to change my appearance at will like a chameleon.* She arranged to study makeup and cosmetics with an expert cosmetician. She became a blue-eyed woman by wearing tinted contact lenses. Soon she felt confident she could become one of three different women if need be, none of whom looked like her CIA photo.

Appearance was only part of the deception. Now she had to give each of her women a different personality. She practiced the three until she believed she was the person she became, like and actor playing a part. Now she had her weapons--the cool sophisticate, the flighty talker, and the sensitive and sensual woman of the world.

* * *

Bill has always been able to leave business at the office, but at home with a lovely wife, who was able to make home life exciting, this day his thoughts were elsewhere. During the time off after SILENT THUNDER he considered the big picture, America was strong once again and getting stronger. Having domesticated the enemy within, the people enjoyed an internal security and contentment it had not felt for generations. Even so, while the threat was no longer within, from the world overseas it was as great a threat as ever.

At home two things were happening before we saw the God-given light once again. First, the gripers and complainers captured the negative media. These people had a habit of making big news out of miner occurrences, causing confidence in our government to wane. Second, the professional politicians fashioned for themselves a paradise not available to the people and nearly spent the nation to death, giving reason for the people to complain. Fortunately the people had enough and finally stood up and recaptured our government and reinstated our Constitution with amendments designed to prevent a return to the abnormal. They finally understood our Constitution was, in George Washington's words, "...a miracle, surely ... written by the finger of God." Therefore, there is no better idea.

Bill understood that we humans must remember the lessons of the Bible and be careful not to interpret the constitution to death—legalism. To understand the intent of the constitution, we must understand the Bible. The spirit of the constitution is clear, but the professional politician would try to circumvent its intent.

What has become known as "the people's non-violent revolution" has set the ship of state back on course. But beyond our shores there are despots who would torpedo it with twisted notions and sinister agendas. Add to that false religious convictions and fanaticism, they pose a clear and present danger not only to Christian America but to the world.

Because of America's military might, our enemies have learned not to wear a uniform but to fight a deadly shadow war of hit-and-run attacks. CSE knows hit-and-run attacks too and has become an effective counter measure against the terrorists. The question is, "Will they ever give up?" The answer is no, not in our lifetime, because in this world there must be evil for the good to overcome. Otherwise we would become soft targets for the evil one. The soft underbelly of society is complacency and apathy because we begin to believe in our own genius instead of a reliance on Almighty God—and God has ways to get our attention. History shows He can play rough when He has to. It is absolutely essential that we be reminded of that from time to time, lest we lose our way and stumble into the abyss. Bill said to Toni, "If only Americans would look beyond their noses to see the implication of their actions we would make far fewer mistakes."

Toni replied, "That's one business fundamental the Bible teaches and the private citizen needs to practice."

"Yes, honesty keeps us in good with the Lord."

Then Toni observed, "Darling, you're so good. Here we are in a quiet evening at home and your thoughts are with our nation and its relationship to God."

"I know, but being at home with you and aware of your obvious attractions only shows how important the subject is in my mind."

Toni thought to herself that the apartment was her turf, and she had to do something to bring him home, to snap him out of his official duty mode in order to fulfill his duty to her.

On the other hand, Bill had learned in there completely honest relationship to read her mind. In a childless marriage they were completely wrapped up in each other and highly sensitive to each other's body language and choice of words. Both were sending an undeniable message to Bill. He asked Toni, "Will it be you or me?"

Taking the lead Toni smiled with a flirtatious grin. "It's my turn to make love, you big hunk of man." Toni had been taught by her mother during her first engagement to make love to her husband often enough and imaginative enough to be sure he could not be tempted by another woman. Yes, that took imagination on her part to keep excitement alive, and much of her leisure time was spent in fantasy to be lived out with her husband so that even if he was so inclined he could not believe there was another Toni in the world. She had been taught well.

It wasn't long until the mother-in-law came to visit. In view of the fact that Bill and Toni's engagement had been brief, she naturally asked if Toni was happy. Their mother-daughter relationship was so close that the phrase "Like mother ... like daughter" seemed most appropriate. However, that didn't include her mother's suspicion of men. As a young wife, her husband had indulged in an affair that led to a kept mistress for over a year. She wondered what to do about it and decided to act as if she knew nothing and ratchet up their sex life. In three months she had regained an honest husband. Toni's glowing praise of Bill was reassuring, but his absences led to mother's suspicions. She decided on a test to ease her mind. Even in her early fifties she was stunningly attractive. Bill was certain Toni would be as beautiful when she was that age.

Bill was on leave and at home during his mother-in-law's visit. One day while Toni was at her office, Mrs. Lopez sat with Bill and began an unusual conversation. "Toni tells me you are the man of all her sexual fantasies. How do you feel about it?"

"As her mother, I can understand your interest in her happiness. All I can say is I feel the same way. She has made it an important part of our marriage, and I'm so glad she taught me how important."

"Yes, she told me how she had to fill you in on that part of your education."

"Oh I was pretty ignorant, but she was a great teacher."

"In my case I was the ignorant one, and it almost cost me my marriage. He was a fine man. But I did not satisfy his need, and he took a mistress. We had spoken frankly about his needs, but I didn't appreciate the power of a young man's sex drive at the time. It wasn't until I made an attempt to save our marriage that I developed a sex drive of my own." Then, looking Bill in the eyes, she said in a low voice, "So much so that after menopause it became even stronger."

"Mrs. Lopez..."

"Call me Vita." Then running her hand through her hair and sliding closer to Bill she said, "Toni told me she had a pile of work at the office and not to wait dinner for her. We have the whole day."

"To do what?"

She lean over to kiss Bill and whispered, "Don't you know, dear?"

Bill stood up, looking back at an apparently relieved Mrs. Lopez and asked, "Why are you doing this? Do you think for a minute I would be unfaithful to Toni with you or any woman?"

Mrs. Lopez suddenly regained her composure and smiled at Bill and complimented, "No. Toni was absolutely right. You are a gem. Please forgive my little test. I had to know."

"Once before I was tempted by an unmarried lady, and I passed the test. It was a test of my faith. Now I'm married, and so are you, so that was not a real test for me. Do you want to know a secret? If we were both single, that would have been a tough test to pass."

"Do you want to know a secret?" She thought to herself how happy she was he didn't accept her offer. "I'm glad you stood up when you did."

Later while Bill was out, Vita and Toni talked in the kitchen,

"Mama, I'm so glad you came for a visit. I hope you can see now the man I fell in love with. He thinks a lot of you."

"Did he say that?"

"Yes, why do you ask?"

"Well, after your comments to me about Bill I began to think about Papa's affair early in our marriage. I know I told you what you must do to avoid the same mistake I made, but I wanted to know two things--firstly if you heeded my advice and secondly if Bill had a roving eye for the ladies?"

"Well?"

"So knowing I was leaving tomorrow, time was short. I decided to put Bill to the test."

"The test, what test?"

"While you were at work I tried to seduce him."

"Mama you didn't!"

"That's right I didn't. His faith in God stood in the way."

"I could have told you that."

"Yes, but now I share your confidence in Bill. I see a lifetime of happiness for you both if--"

"If what?"

"...you continue to fulfill his needs."

"My needs will take care of that."

"Keep that thought. Do you know what he said to me? 'Don't worry, that daughter of yours is all I can handle."

"Mama, compared to Bill the grass is all dried up on the other side of the fence."

"I'm happy for you dear. I'll be happy to get home. I need papa as much as you need Bill and in the same way he needs me."

"I can imagine that homecoming. Go to it mama."

* * *

It was between missions for Bill and becoming SPIRIT once again he checked into MAGNOLIA to catch up on intelligence summaries and to do some necessary research. The summaries seemed to broadcast an alarm to track down and arrest a female

KGB agent who had infiltrated the CIA. The entire organization was on the alert and finding her was top priority. Catching up, he read dated summaries until he was current on the situation. She had disappeared behind the Iron Curtain and was likely to stay there—too much was known about her. SPIRIT reasoned that in time the search would cool off and there might be the day when she would become the target for CSE. He thought for a few moments and tried to put himself in her place as an agent. Being a woman, she would be less conspicuous than a man if she remained in character and didn't act like a man. Her network would have women close to her and men on the fringes. That way she would be insulated from the obvious. She would be just one of the girls. Anyway at present there are more likely scenarios to take under study. He shifted his attention to more realistic and immediate considerations.

As a licensed pilot Bill purchase a plane to commute between Washington and Atlanta—a gift from Toni, who expressed the desire that he fly to her on wings of love. At each end of the commute was a small private airfield where he kept a car in order to keep his frequent comings and goings inconspicuous. When he arrived at their apartment, Bill saw a yellow ribbon tied in a bow to the door knocker. He entered to find a yellow ribbon attached to the door latch with a note, "Follow the yellow ribbon". After he picked up a pair of Toni's shoes, he was guided to the dining room and another note that read, "Man does not live by bread alone". Grasping her skirt, he continued and was led by the ribbon to the living room, where he found her blouse and bra with another note. "You're getting hot so keep going." The ribbon led to the bathroom, and the note said, "Just in case, keep going." Then on the bedroom door another note read: "The portal to ecstasy. Don't knock." Bill opened the door and gazed on sheer beauty in a near transparent negligee. Toni basked for a moment in his gaze and then asked, "What are you doing dressed? I thought you'd be dropping clothes every time you saw one of mine."

"Next time I'll know better. Your lack of modesty encourages mine."

"I thought by now you'd think of it as complete and loving surrender of my body to yours."

"I see a new application to the phrase "What's really important is what you learn after you think you know it all.""

At this Toni pulled a tie and her negligee fell to the floor. "Shut up. Come here."

Bill had many reasons to be thankful for the life he was living--a job that satisfied his need to serve, a life's companion who understood him and offered him an intimate and fulfilling marriage, and all the time feeling he was doing God's work. The harmony of their religious convictions caused Bill to look upon Toni as God's reward for his obedience. A dangerous job yes, but he understood that as long as he was true and kept his wits about him God was his protection.

CHAPTER 12

BORN AGAIN

A secret CIA research and cryptographic unit occupied the twenty-sixth floor of a building at 73 Friederich Strasse in Schweinfurt, Germany. The CIA owned the building and leased space through a dummy corporation to legitimate firms. The twenty-sixth floor was known to its occupants as "the penthouse" and was reachable only by a concealed elevator and stairwell from the vacant twenty-fifth floor. The unit was staffed by talented academic types trained to find the connection between seemingly unrelated bits of information and to break codes.

Bud Liu and Roy Jones were professional cryptanalysts working together on a knotty problem. There wasn't much they didn't know about codes and ciphers. What they didn't know didn't take long to unravel. Elaborate code machines such as Germany's Enigma were not suitable for agents in the field who were constantly on the move. Simple codes were devised which would delay the enemy so that by the time it was deciphered the action had already occurred. Liu and Jones uncovered a KGB cell operating in the area but had not located it.

What the CIA didn't know was the KGB cell they sought was made up of several women and a few men and headed by COUGAR. The women agent's cover were activities normally conducted by women, visiting boutiques, beauty salons, art galleries, and hospitals, where the comings and goings of women were routine and would not seem unusual; however, the cell was the Europe section of Department V, and the COUGAR was on the loose. She was herself when with her people, but with others assumed the character of a dumb blond. No one would guess she had the intelligence and ability of a successful assassin. The men in her cell were decoys acting suspiciously like enemy agents but in reality accomplishing no great harm. Surveillance of them would keep the CIA busy and keep the western nations from learning of the dangerous cell and its real purpose. The decoys knew nothing of the activities of the rest of the cell so if caught, no harm done. Insulated from detection by these precautions, COUGAR was free to "get her hands dirty."

Liu and Jones continued to assemble the pieces of the puzzle. Bit by bit the picture was becoming clear. Bud Liu finally found the key piece and the picture was near completion--enough to reach a disturbing conclusion.

It didn't take long for this intelligence to reach the president. An assassination plot was in the works, but of whom and by who was the question. EVEREST saw a possible CSE action should the opportunity present itself and alerted CLIMBER to be prepared for a possible mission directive. Both Task Teams HAMMER and SPIRIT were told to direct their research to Germany and possible CSE involvement.

His extensive research led SPIRIT to a definite conclusion. Comparing our history to that of Europe emphasized the glaring differences between us. Uniting the comparatively small area that is Europe has been the dream of the peace makers of history, but the one ingredient that unites a people is a common language. A relatively small geographical area that speaks seven or more languages is next to impossible to unite. A single language is required to unite a single country. Europe's history has been bloody for centuries—war after war. SPIRIT saw the reverse happening in America, which became the great nation of The United States because we were united by one language. Yet today we are becoming multilingual and more and more divided and polarized, sapping our strength as a nation. We have twice pulled Europe's chess nuts out of the fire at great cost to our younger generation. America must insist that to become a naturalized citizen it is necessary to pass an English test—both written and oral. It may even be necessary to report people overheard speaking a foreign tongue so that they may be forcibly enrolled in English classes or leave the country—foreign tourist the exception.

EVEREST and CLIMBER examined the latest intelligence summaries which clarified earlier incomplete reports of the pending assassination attempt. Reliable sources identified the victim and the group responsible. Neither were a threat to the United States, and it was determined that normally our only responsibility was to warn the intended victim. EVEREST and CLIMBER agreed that in this case it was in our best interest not to meddle in the internal affairs of the country in question, not even to warn the oppressive victim. Therefore, a mission directive was not forthcoming, but CLIMBER decided to let the task teams continue their research just in case. Events indicated unrest in the area, and it was best to be ready for any circumstance that might call for CSE deployment. Later the president's decision was justified because as it turned out the group behind the assassination plot was supported by the CIA. The group had long awaited the opportunity. No one knew when the chance would come. When it finally did come, even the CIA was surprised at the persistence of the group. Fortunately the time lag had no adverse effect on American interests.

However, another situation arose which would have an adverse effect on American interests if something wasn't done about it—and soon. CSE was alerted to be ready for a mission directive. However, tardy intelligence caused the president to realize the events had moved too fast, and the situation no longer lend itself to CSE intervention. It would be out of character for a CSE operation and threatened exposure of nation's best kept secret. Therefore the president wisely cancelled the alert and directed action by other agencies.

Owing to the recent actions of the American people, the business of efficient government moved on to new heights. However, the president felt that the failures of past administrations were partly due to poor communication with the people, leading to suspicions and misunderstandings. Under this circumstance, the erroneous criticisms were given credibility. To correct this critical error, the president issued an executive order giving him authority to preempt scheduled broadcasting in order to address the people of the nation. He knew this action would bring network executives to the conference table. He assured them he would not abuse the privilege. To his surprise, the networks had already discussed the problem and offered the president a solution which was mutually beneficial. He would reach the people regularly, and the networks would get periodic updates. They offered the president a monthly one hour primetime slot for executive use. Seizing the opportunity, the president pressed for all the networks to air the broadcasts simultaneously and reminded them that their licenses to broadcast were at the courtesy of the government of the people, by the people and for the people and programming must be held to a high moral standard or risk forfeiting their license. Further, commercialism was to be second priority to quality programming.

The purpose of his monthly broadcasts was to capture the interest of the people in their government and emphasize the *why* of government actions. The president's broadcast style was relaxed in a friend to friend fashion reminiscent of the Roosevelt fireside chats. Networks were reminded they were a public service and encouraged to present all sides of issues of the day. Editors were told to familiarize themselves with the US Constitution and to oppose any law or regulation that appeared in conflict.

Opposing and supporting opinion would be confined to a clearly designated editorial segment of every scheduled news broadcast.

Weeks in advance the president's inaugural monthly chat was advertised by means of fifteen to thirty-second spots on radio, TV, and ads in syndicated newspapers across the nation. This unprecedented media blitz created the public curiosity it sought. Across the nation in small-town barber shops to big city-restaurants, the talk was of the president's town hall meeting with the nation. Speculation was rife as to the subject of his broadcast. Never before has a government initiative captured such interest, and anticipation was high.

Finally, on the second Tuesday night of the month, the presidential seal appeared on the TV sets worldwide. Yes, because of the citizen's revolution, the world had become interested in the democratic process. A familiar, trusted, and distinguished voice introduced the new monthly presidential radio and TV series and invited the listening and viewing audience to quiet down and visit with their president. But still there was no mention of the subjects to be discussed. The presidential seal dissolved to the president dressed casually and sitting in front of a blazing fireplace in the Oval Office. The voice-over, departing from tradition, introduced, "America, here is your president."

The president, sitting in an easy chair with a white loose leaf binder in his lap, looked up, smiled, and said, "Good evening, friends. This is the first of many regular conversations we'll have during my administration. I say conversations because you can participate by writing me here at the White House with your questions and comments, which I will endeavor to answer on my next broadcast. Not individually of course, but many will address the same subject, and I'll do my best to clarify the issue for you.

"You sent me here to do a job that desperately needed to be done, and I see this as my monthly report to you on its progress. We have come a long way in a short time. The constitutional convention has cured a lot of what ailed us. Even so, there is still a glaring problem that a nation under God needs to address.

In many ways we are born again, a new nation, and as with our Founding Fathers, we must begin with God's blessing. A nation cannot be truly born again unless the people, who are the nation, are also born again. I recognize that some of you might be thinking, *Why bring God into politics?* Bear with me. This is no sermon. Just remember God's ethics makes honest men and women in all spheres of life. I'm going to reveal life-changing information to complete your education. As Noah Webster said, 'Education is useless without the Bible.'

"To create a better citizenry we must ask three questions: Who are we as a people? From where did we come? And where are we headed? The answers to those vital questions are found in a study of our history as a people.

"Let me show you what our Founding Fathers, partners with God in creating these United States, believed and why. First, these men were leaders in the thirteen colonies. Going back as far as the Pilgrim Fathers, their purpose in making the dangerous voyage on a tiny ship named the Mayflower, announced in the Mayflower Compact, was to escape religious persecution and to advance the Christian faith in the new world. They made friends of the Native Americans and purchased land from them, and in turn the natives helped them survive that severe first winter in the new land. In the decades that followed before the Declaration of Independence and the first constitutional convention all children were taught to read from the Bible. The alphabet was taught with letters being the first letter of Bible verses. The first colleges were Christian institutions, such as Harvard, Princeton, and the University of Pennsylvania. Graduates of these schools went on to create other Christian institutions of higher learning. Is it any wonder that these men looked to God for divine assistance in creating a new nation? So our Founding Fathers, who are generally thought to be the signers of Declaration of Independence and the Constitution, looked to God for guidance in creating a great document, filled with provisions taken directly from the Holy Scriptures. To illustrate the overriding priority of our delegates to the convention let me quote some important statements which are so plentiful because these were learned men, products of a Christian education. First, in answer to the question, what is the role of faith in public life, George Washington said to the governors of the states June 8, 1783,

> I now make it my earnest prayer that God would have you and the State over which you preside, in His holy protection, that he would incline the hearts of the citizens to cultivate a spirit of subordination and obedience to government; to entertain a brotherly affection and love for one another, for their fellow citizens of the United States at large, and particularly for their brethren who have served in the field; and, finally, that he would be most graciously pleased to dispose us all to do justice, to love mercy, and to demean ourselves with that charity, and pacific temper of mind, which were characteristic of the Divine Author of our blessed religion, and without an humble imitation of whose example in these things we can never hope to be a happy nation.

> 'In his second inaugural address, George Washington also said, 'Our constitution is a miracle, surely it was written by the finger of God.'

> "In his notes on the state of Virginia, Thomas Jefferson said, God who gave us life gave us liberty. And can the liberties of a nation be thought to be secure when we have removed their only firm basis, a conviction in the minds of the people that these liberties are a Gift of God; that they are not to be violated but with His wrath? Indeed, I tremble for my country when I reflect that God is just; that His justice cannot sleep forever

In 1778, James Madison said to the general assembly of the state of Virginia, 'We have staked the whole future of American civilization, not upon the power of government, far from it. We've staked the future of all political institutions upon our capacity ... to sustain ourselves according to the Ten Commandments of God.'

"It may interest you to learn that our Pledge of Allegiance was first written in 1892 by a Baptist minister from Boston named Francis Bellamy. The words "under God" were taken from Abraham Lincoln's famous Gettysburg Address, "that this nation, under God, shall have a new birth." In my mind, friends, we have today by our actions to set things straight have undergone a new birth, a Gift of God. This gift is like the seed in a parable of Jesus, the seed which was received with joy but could not sink roots because the ground was hard and dry ... or the seed that landed in the thorns and thistles and was choked to death by the problems of everyday life. These seeds died because they were not cultivated. So our faith dies or is weakened because it is not the priority in our lives, resulting in our believing false prophets who would destroy us. No matter how lofty our social position or how heinous our crimes God will forgive those who ask.

Queen Victoria, the longest reigning monarch in history (1837-1901), said, 'I long so to lay my crown at the feet of Jesus.'

In 1757, Benjamin Franklin said, 'Work as if you were to live 100 years; pray as if you were to die tomorrow.'

"My last quotation on the power of God tonight goes to the heart of the proposition I put to you tonight. To secure God's blessing we must be a pious nation. Listen to Thomas Jefferson again. He said this on March 23, 1801,

The Christian Religion, when divested of the rags in which they (the clergy) have enveloped it, and brought to the original purity and simplicity of its benevolent institutor (Jesus), is a religion of all others most friendly to liberty, science, and the freest expansion of the human mind.

"Let us turn now to our personal behavior. As a Christian nation, we are to love our neighbor as ourselves. If we don't love ourselves, we haven't the capacity to love others. If you don't love yourself, you have a deep seated reason. That reason lives inside you like a cancer and will lead to an early grave. To cut out that cancer, you must face it, admit it, and ask God to forgive it. Jesus bore all your sins to the cross. When you know that and ask God to forgive you and make every attempt to sin no more, then you have become His child and are welcomed into the family of God. All have violated the Ten Commandments many times. The Bible views the Ten Commandments as one law with ten parts, so if you violate one part, you have violated the law. Christ's sacrifice was to save you and me. Personally, I'm forever grateful.

"Jesus told the adulteress to sin no more. Some imagine that to be a difficult challenge. Here's some help from Benjamin Franklin, who wrote in his *Maxims and Morals* lessons for life,

'Search others for their virtues, thy self for thy vices.

Keep your eyes open before marriage, half shut afterwards.

My father convinced me that nothing was useful which was not honest.

Freedom is not a gift bestowed upon us by others, but a right that belongs to us by the laws of God and nature.

Virtue alone is sufficient to make a man great, glorious and happy.

Let the fair sex be assured that I shall always treat them and their affairs with utmost decency and respect.

Self-denial is really the highest self-gratification.

Beware of little expenses.

I never doubted the existence of the Deity; that he made the world, and governed it by His Providence.

Good wives and good plantations are made by good husbands.

Hope and faith may be more firmly grounded upon Charity than Charity upon hope and faith.

Virtue is not secure until its practice has become habitual.

Nothing is so likely to make a man's fortune as virtue.

Without virtue man can have no happiness.

The pleasures of this world are rather from God's goodness than our own merit.

Contrary habits must be broken, and good ones acquired and established, before we can have any dependence on a steady, uniform rectitude of conduct. Let no pleasure tempt you, no profit allure you, no ambition corrupt you, no example sway you, no persuasion move you to do anything you know to be evil; so you shall live jollily, for a good conscience is a continual Christmas.'

"I can't end this lesson in moral behavior without a word from Abraham Lincoln who said, 'Nothing is politically right which is morally wrong.'

"In future broadcasts I'll address the important issues of the day, but I feel the most important issue we face today is our relationship with God. As 'one nation under God,' there is nothing more important than His blessing. I'm not ashamed to tell my friends that their education is incomplete without the Bible. The first thing you must learn is your body will die sooner or later, but your spirit, your soul, will never die. You won't find another mortal body to live in. You will go to a place you have chosen by your behavior in this mortal lifetime—heaven or hell. If up to now you haven't chosen to follow Jesus, take warning. You haven't much time left. Satan is watching and rubbing his hands ready to hustle you off to the fires of hell. Even so, Jesus is standing by with the key to the kingdom in His hand, but he won't give it to you. You must reach out and take it by asking forgiveness for your sins and inviting Jesus into your heart. The door to your heart has no outside knob so the only way Jesus can enter is for you to open it from the inside. Once you do you are saved.

"I said in the beginning we have come a long way together in curing the ills of our beloved country. In the past we as a people have been shown to have a short memory. Without a strong faith in God, I fear a relapse. Don't let that happen. Find a Bible-believing church and attend it regularly for spiritual support and moral strength. However, be certain the pastor teaches the Bible, not some feel good theology. Remember the words of Jesus who said, 'I am the way, the truth and the life; no one comes to the father but by me.' And, 'If you have seen me you have seen the Father.'

"We have shown the world what a free people can do when obeying God's law and a God-inspired Constitution."

At this point the scene changed to a live shot of the Statue of Liberty and the voice-over was the president's, "It seems to me

Miss Liberty's light shines a little brighter tonight. Good night until next time. God bless you all and your families."

* * *

Reaction to the president's "chat" was positive and tagged by the media as the president's "Born Again Speech." If reaction at home was positive, overseas missionaries were amazed and thankful for a powerful message from the President of the United States, which attracted great interest among people they had been trying to reach for years. The fact that the most powerful man on earth was a Christian contradicted what they had been told by atheist that Christians were superstitious simpletons, prompting missionaries to point out that most famous (as opposed to infamous) figures in history were Christians--men and women who were leaders in their specific fields of endeavor. Churches in America suddenly had a parking problem. Crusades filled stadiums nationwide. TV networks were overwhelmed with requests for quality Christian films, which, to the surprise of network officials, were plentiful and readily available. The unexpected response testified to the hunger in the human breast for hope and freedom to worship God. In just a few months much of the world's population felt the weight of oppression lifted from their backs. News media spoke of nations taking a close look at their own constitution and comparing them with ours. Respect for America spiraled upward. Established Christians saw God at work in a powerful way. A strong America had shown its strength in a spiritual way making her strength complete.

* * *

Having witnessed the president's chat COUGAR was confused and upset. She thought that in no way did the president attack her convictions. He expressed his own in a clear and illuminating fashion. She recalled vague childhood memories of her introduction to the Russian Orthodox Church, which the revolution stifled, and tried to see similarities between what she could remember and what the president said. Something clicked in her mind, and she became curious, but she had work to do that had nothing to do with spiritual matters. As days went by, she was distracted by an obsession to know more about what was promised to be a better way to live. She was eager to know more, but the question holding her back was would God forgive the long list of heinous crimes she had committed, the level of evil she had reached? Before any other considerations she had to know the answer to that question. To find out, she'd go to the source, so she made an appointment with a Protestant pastor in Schweinfurt at a restaurant so she would not feel intimidated by church surroundings.

Pastor Hans Muller earned his doctoral degree at a theological seminary in the United States. As a young communist spy in East Germany, he had defected when he realized the error of communism's flight from God. The reunification of Germany bought him home to preach to a needy people. His church was large and influential in the community, mainly because of his God-given powers of persuasion. Because of his experience with Soviet communism, he understood the hardness and stick-to-business attitude in COUGAR as they sat over lunch. COUGAR introduced herself in fluent German as Frau Steinbach to cover her accent. Small talk prevailed until they had finished eating. Then he wiped his mouth with a napkin and recognized the accent, Dr. Muller commented, "This is my favorite place, I come here often. The food is good at reasonable prices. Now, what can I do for you?"

Being in a public place they spoke in low tones. COUGAR began, "Did you hear the speech by the American president?"

"Who didn't?" Dr. Muller felt comfortable with the prospect of helping Katrina Romanov with her problem. Despite the passing years he recognized her as a fellow KGB agent in his youth. She apparently didn't recognize him, but his bearing and expression seem to have a relaxing effect on her. She could, within limits, be open and frank with him.

"I was moved by his message and at the same time ashamed."

"Ashamed? About what?"

"About my past."

"Alright, what about your past?"

"Sinful. So sinful I doubt if there is anyone in the world as evil as me."

"Why do you say that?"

"If I were to take the president's message seriously there is a high wall of sin barring my way to salvation."

Dr. Muller paused in thought. *If she is still a KGB agent I understand her meaning.* Then he asked, "Let's look at what you think to be your most serious sin. What would that be?"

"Murder."

"Oh. What were the circumstances?"

She waited hesitant to reveal her secret. Several seconds of silence passed and then she said, "Assassination."

"On your own or by what authority?"

"I work for my government."

"The Soviets?"

"Yes."

"Do you want to tell me more of your work?"

"I can't."

Dr. Muller lean forward and looked her in the eyes and said, "Katrina?"

She stiffened in surprise and said, "Who are you?"

"I am an ordained minister of the Gospel, formerly an agent of the KGB. Do you remember me? It was a long time ago? We trained together, but we never worked together. I defected for reasons of my faith and went to school in the United States. So you see I understand your position. Shall we go on?"

"Yes."

"OK, I understand you killed, it doesn't matter how many times."

At this point, speaking of Christian doctrine, he spoke in a normal tone of voice and was overheard by nearby patrons.

"The Bible teaches that the Ten Commandments are in fact one commandment, God's law, because if you violate one you violate all because you have broken God's law. One is no less important than the others. Jesus added a new commandment--that you love one another as yourself. If you cannot love yourself, you cannot love others, and that will keep you from God. However--and this is the core of our faith--Jesus Christ took your sins upon Himself and became sin dying on the cross and descended into hell only to rise again three days later to be seen and spoken to by about five hundred followers before ascending to the Father before their very eyes. Your sins are forgiven only if you are a follower of Christ, and you demonstrate that by asking His forgiveness of your sins and asking Jesus to take residence in your heart of hearts. By doing that. you become a child of God and your sins--past, present, and future--are forgiven. When you have done that, you have a clean slate, a new life, and the ability to love the new person you have become and therefore others."

Six people from tables nearby had paid rapt attention to his last statement and rose from their tables and came him to give their hearts to the Lord. The "Iron Duchess" became the seventh child of God in that public place and departed with her mentor. The KGB still cannot explain the why or where of her disappearance. I have only explained the why.

CHAPTER 13

DEFECTION

D octor Muller was grateful for the American president's strong stand on Christianity and its powerful impact on the German people and was moved to tell him so, but now he had a responsibility toward Katrina Romanov. She expressed the desire to attend the same seminary as the Pastor. She had confessed all to him, including the fact that she was the subject of a worldwide arrest warrant because it was discovered she had infiltrated the CIA. She told her mentor that in the short time as a mole agent she had done no harm and passed no CIA secrets to the KGB. Moreover, she asked the good pastor to vouch for her request for political asylum in the United States.

Dr. Muller was torn between her confession and the realization that if Katrina Romanov had a sinister agenda and truly not had a change of heart, his life could be forfeited because of the new information she had given him. But for the life of him he couldn't see an evil motive for her coming to him in the first place. In the days after her conversion she took refuge in the church, and her only interest was in the word of God. Their discussions were confined to the Holy Scriptures, and her retention and understanding of the basics of Christian doctrine was impressive. He could only guide her and trust God to change her. It appeared that He was doing a good job of it. She was full of questions and approached her studies with a scholarly enthusiasm and curiosity. It seemed her appetite for God's word was insatiable. He didn't see any danger in trusting her, so he composed a personal letter to the president.

To: The President of the United States

The White House

Washington, D.C. USA

From: Hans Muller, Doctor of Divinity,

Pastor, First Assembly of God Church

Schweinfurt, Germany

Dear Mr. President,

Hearty congratulations on your inspiring talk with the American people; on which most of the world was privileged to eavesdrop.

Your message reached a surprising audience. It touched the heart of a KGB agent operating here in Schweinfurt. She is not unknown to you since there is a warrant for her arrest because she infiltrated your Central Intelligence Agency. In her short time as a mole she did no harm and passed no secrets to the KGB because her control and link to the Kremlin code name KRAIT had been killed. Before she could accept your message, she had to have the answer to the question which held her and many others back. Would God forgive her evil?

Katrina Romanov is a middle aged woman who has served the Soviets for many years and has personally murdered to achieve her ends. After viewing your TV broadcast, she felt ashamed and thought no one could be as evil as she. She came to me for answers and received the Lord in her heart. I am confident of that. She has taken sanctuary in the church and has diligently studied the Holy Scriptures. As a youth and defected KGB agent myself, I knew her then and understand and trust her now. If I am wrong, I know too much about her to live, but I'm positive I am right about her. She requests political asylum in the United States and desires to attend the seminary I attended for my doctorate. I sincerely believe God has changed her heart and I thank you, Mr. President, for her inspiration. She is not the first to come to me for council since your broadcast. You have set a fine example for other leaders to help create a better, more loving world.

Anticipate your reply and instruction with respect to her request for asylum. She is prepared to give herself up to the United States Consulate here.

Sincerely yours in Christ,

Hans Muller, DD

* * *

The president read the letter three times and felt good about it, not only the compliment but about the defection of a Soviet agent who had apparently seen the light. It would be up to the CIA and others to verify her motives before asylum could be granted. She could not be held personally responsible for her misdeeds, except to God, as long as they were to accomplish a mission directed by her government. He notified the CIA and directed the State Department to alert our Embassy in Berlin of the defection of a Soviet KGB agent named Katrina Romanov and to contact Dr. Hans Muller, pastor of the First Assembly of God church in Schweinfurt who had given her sanctuary.

The newly assigned Military Attaché Colonel George Morley read the messages fresh from the decoder. This morning he was intrigued by the alert message. He asked himself why a defecting agent from a godless country would have anything to do with the clergy. He instructed his secretary to call Pastor Muller, whose church Colonel Morley had just begun to attend in Berlin.

Colonel Morley's secretary informed him she had Pastor Muller on the line.

"Pastor Muller?"

"Yes."

"I am Colonel Morley, Military Attaché at the American Embassy ... and a new member of your branch church here in Berlin. I understand we have a mutual interest, so I'd like to travel to Schweinfurt and pick up you and our mutual interest and bring you here."

"Yes, what time?"

"In two hours?"

"That would be fine. Tell your driver to use the back alley entrance; there is a crowd out front."

"I understand, goodbye."

Colonel Morley arrived at the church on time. Dr. Muller and his companion moved quickly to the car.

"Good morning pastor, ma'am."

Doctor Muller replied,

"Good morning. For two days now there has been two men watching the front entrance. Katrina recognized them so that's why the back entrance."

The Colonel, who had fought the Cold War from the beginning, thought for a moment that he was now face to face with the enemy. Then he thought, *Could this be a legitimate opportunity to employ the biblical admonition to forgive your enemy?* Then he said, "You'll be safe under our protection. You ma'am will stay at the embassy for the immediate future. I have arranged an interview with members of the CIA in about two hours. Your initial acceptance will be their responsibility. Then you'll be flown to a safe house near Washington. Upon your arrival your arrest warrant will be cancelled."

During her interrogation at the embassy she was asked how she came to the decision to defect. Her answer was forthright and clear. "All my life I sought acceptance and had a strong need to belong. I thought I had found both in my work. I dedicated myself to the cause of communism and was accepted as a skillful agent. Still, there was another need I didn't understand. That bothered me. I looked for answers in many ways—mostly sinful. Over time my actions and methods became more despicable until I stopped at nothing to succeed in my mission—murder, sex and deceit. It all seemed to me that the end justified the means. I became recognized as an effective agent in the KGB, but when I looked in the mirror, I didn't like what I saw. I had to admit that deep down I hated what I had become. It wasn't love of country that made me do these things. It was my hate of people and my selfish ambition.

"Then I sank into a period of depression. I thought all these years have come to this. What's the use? I was in just the emotional condition to find the answer in the telecast of the US president's message. One phrase resonated in my heart, 'Jesus gave us a new commandment to love one another as you love yourself. If you cannot love yourself, you can't love others. To be born again is to begin again—a new life.' But my evil was so terrible. How could God forgive me? I didn't know the first step for a sinner to become a Christian can be described in four key words: *I now forgive myself.* In the next few days I thought of nothing else. I had to have an answer if I was to believe, so I found Pastor Muller, and here I am seeking political asylum and spiritual freedom."

Her eyes became tearful, "Jesus is my Lord and my God."

Her interrogators were silent. Then drying her tears she said, "I ask for asylum in the U.S. because a nation with a leader like yours is where I want to live and learn."

CHAPTER 14

CAUTIOUS HELP

O ne of Bill Bowman's favorite forms of relaxation, when apart from Toni, is slipping on headphones and listening to the music of the masters and popular classics by singers who sing instead of shout. Rock and roll is anything but relaxing. He sees it a noise pollution with a beat. Rock concerts are more about beat and decibel levels creating a generation of the hard of hearing.

Next on his list of relaxing events is the game of golf, a four to five mile walk with the lessons of life. Most duffers cheat at the game, breaking the rules openly or in secret—like life. The rule most violated is moving the ball to a better lie before stroking it, and not calling a penalty on oneself. He compared the rule with taking what comes in life and making the most of it. The Bible tells us the road to destruction is broad and filled with hazards but the road to heaven is straight and narrow. There is a saying in golf, "Stay in the short grass." A good golfer hits accurate shots neither too far to the left nor to the right, but even the best miss the fairway now and then. When they do, they wind up in the woods, the rough, or sand bunkers. Many times it costs them an extra stroke or more. They pay the penalty for missing the narrow fairway. Golfer or not we must pay the penalty for wandering from the straight and narrow. The narrow road represents Christianity and is the safe route. The Scots are a religious people, and they developed the game to teach the lessons of life. Develop the skill and obey the rules, or in everyday life, be good at your job and obey God's law. Up to now this philosophy had put Bill to the test many times in his army career, and he has passed with flying colors. He lived always expecting new tests, which were sure to come.

Bill had read Lloyd C. Douglas' book *Magnificent Obsession* and took it to heart. It recalled passages in the Bible which said that doing good deeds in public only gets you earthly rewards, but doing them in secret builds your treasure in heaven. In spite of his dangerous occupation he felt truly free, and doing God's work gave him a sense of spiritual fulfillment. He also realized his work was a privilege not granted to most, and he was grateful for the opportunity. When preparing for a mission he had this thought in mind. When you have used all your professional skill and brains, there comes a time when you must turn events over to God, and leave them there. He credits that thought to his hero, General of the Armies Dwight David Eisenhower.

A colleague once told Bill, "You don't seem to have any problems in your life."

To which he replied, "Oh, I've had problems all right, but God has taught me a better way to handle them. We cannot see into the future, but obedience to the word of God gives us the way to prepare for it. I always try to remember that Satan puts a question mark where God puts a period."

At MAGNOLIA, SPIRIT was relaxing while listening to *Les Preludes by Franz Liszt* when WIZARD tapped him on the shoulder. Pulling off his headphones he responded, "Yes sir?"

"I've just fingered you for a job. What do you know about San Pedro?" SPIRIT paused for a moment before answering, "The country or the city?"

"The country."

"South American republic, coffee, bananas, the president is Juan Ortega...a benevolent leader of a country populated mostly by peasants. He was an army colonel who led a bloodless coup twenty-one years ago."

"Good, that's a start. Ortega visited Washington to confer with the president but was called home to handle a serious problem. We don't know what that problem was or is, so discussion was brief, and almost in passing he indicated that U.S. help would be welcome. In his haste it was mutually agreed to talk later.

"Returning from the airport EVEREST called for the latest CIA intelligence summaries, subject San Pedro. He learned that after the coup, twenty-one years ago, Ortega instituted needed reforms and the country settled into a period of peace and quiet ... until recently. We can't understand why, but it looks like a violent revolution is in the offing. Terrorism has replaced open warfare as the primary weapon. Ortega has marshaled his forces but has had little effect on the hit-and-run tactics of the terrorists.

"Now he has formally asked for our help in training his army to fight a war on terrorism. Naturally EVEREST is cautious. He doesn't want to involve the army Special Forces until he is sure of the situation and its perils if any. In order to keep from being drawn into a situation that could be embarrassing to the United States, he wants sound information upon which to make a decision. You, my friend, have been handed the mission. What is your first reaction to the order?"

"The first thought that strikes me is I can't use my entire team because only three speak Spanish. On a mission of this nature the entire team must speak the language, so I have to borrow from the other teams."

"Done, what else?"

"We'll go in organized like a Special Forces A Team, but in civilian clothes of course, and as we teach and during time off, we'll ask discreet questions and keep our eyes and ears open. How long do we have to prepare?"

"How long do you need?"

"At least a week."

"EVEREST said he'd like to deploy you in a couple of weeks, so we're okay there."

"We'll spend most of that time sharpening our linguistic skills and reviewing pertinent facts about the country."

"Good, I'll have all the Spanish speaking members of CSE in the conference room tomorrow morning for you to interview and to select seven to fill out your team. I'll notify EVEREST of your selection as leader and that you'll be ready in two weeks."

EVEREST, speaking on the phone to President Ortega, announced that he would have a counter terrorist instructor team ready to arrive in San Pedro in two weeks. Ortega sounded agitated and explained the urgent need for help and insisted on an earlier arrival. EVEREST replied, "The best I can do is one week."

"Very well, that will have to do. Thank you, sir."

SPIRIT briefed his tailored team on an unusual mission, which he dubbed operation CAUTIOUS HELP. Similar to Special Forces but dressed as civilians, they were to gather information about the situation in order to satisfy EVEREST's uneasiness. Both on and off duty, they were to ask questions like tourists in search of specific answers. If there was more here than meets the eye, EVEREST wanted to know about it. They were to be dumb tourists enjoying themselves, while at the same time they were smart spies on an important mission. Of course they would use assumed names as they did in operation ARROW II.

SPIRIT was Edward Miller. H2 was Carlos Diaz. S34 was Robert Bright. T24 was Guy Martinez. S42 was David Randall. T26 was Juan Hernandez. S51 was John Kellogg. M44 was Felix Fernando. H57 was Jose Maderas. Finally M45 was Aldo Moreno.

Upon arrival at San Pedro International Airport the team was greeted by President Ortega himself, and they boarded a first class tour bus. Mr. Miller rode with the president in his bullet proof presidential limousine. For a poor country the capitol was opulent. Obviously most of the wealth of the country was here.

It looked as if coffee and bananas were a good investment. Miller felt his studies misled him—another reason to ask questions. As the limousine turned a corner they came upon a fire, what was left of a car bombing. Buildings were damaged, and store windows shattered. Several bodies lay dead and wounded in the street. As if trained or experienced in this situation, the driver expertly avoided the bodies and accelerated to high speed.

"Mr. Miller, you see what I am up against here. Could you have prevented that?"

"Perhaps, but at least we will teach you some tricks to fight back effectively."

Seated in the limo with them was a man introduced as the president's secretary of agriculture. Miller wondered what interest the secretary would have in his mission, but said nothing.

"Mr. Miller, I have assigned Senor Fernandez as your guide while you are with us."

Miller thought to himself, *My guide or my guard?* They soon arrived at the presidential palace, a citadel of grandeur. It looked as if it had been built less than twenty-one years ago—opulent indeed. Armed guards were stationed so that all sides of the building could be observed.

"You and your men will be safe here, Mr. Miller. During off-duty hours, feel free to tour our capitol. Your bus parked over there will give you secure transportation to and from the city center. The terrorists have not as yet dared operate inside the city center. Using any other transportation will not guarantee your safety. So let us go in. I think you'll find the accommodations comfortable and the food first-rate."

The next morning after a grand buffet breakfast, Miller asked, "What time do we leave for army headquarters, Mr. President?"

"We don't. I have selected twelve of my most trusted officers to attend class right here. That will maintain secrecy and be absolutely secure. After you're gone, they will return to their units and train them."

"Mr. President, the final phase of our training schedule is a field exercise to put into practice what the students have learned with our supervision. It's very important."

"But not necessary. These officers are bright and imaginative. You can be sure they will put to effective use what you have taught them."

The alarm bell of suspicion sounded loud and clear in Miller's mind. He felt like a trustee prisoner with limited freedom—but why? If given the freedom to roam the countryside, what might they find? Coffee and bananas, but what else? Training limited to closed classrooms in the presidential compound began the next day. It was a convenient set-up, but not as effective as it should be. Ortega insisted on a schedule of two days training and one day off, but would not give a reason. With surveillance and listening devices everywhere, Miller had to be careful in communicating his feelings to the team. Aboard the bus to the city he suggested they split up in pairs and meet for lunch at a restaurant, a different place each time, to compare notes on the best places to visit. This sounded reasonable to Senor Fernandez, and he offered no objection. This gave the team the opportunity to question the local populace. Not being able to accompany the entire group, Fernandez decided to stay with the driver in the parked bus and enjoy a siesta. Having recommended a restaurant, he planned to join them for lunch unannounced. As they left the bus, Miller passed out tourist guide books in which he had circled a different restaurant in which to meet. At lunch he was free to speak for the first time since their arrival and spoke of his suspicions and explained his reason for splitting into two-man teams.

"On the assumption that Ortega has something to hide, I want you all to engage the locals in conversation asking discreet questions. I know you are all skilled in two-man interrogation, so frame your questions as a tourist's curiosity. Flatter them and show admiration of their beautiful capitol city, which could not have been built on the sweat of the peasants. Get the idea? Draw them out. Get them talking about any aspect of their society. We are looking for information that would be useful to us and to EVEREST. It's obvious we are under surveillance in the palace so our only chance to confer is these luncheons. Questions?"

Diaz raised his hand and asked, "What do you think Ortega is hiding?"

Miller replied thoughtfully, "I don't know. It's too early to tell, but I can't shake the feeling it's something significant. You would do well to think the same thing in your questioning."

The team's third trip to town revealed some surprising and startling information which answered more questions than were asked. Three of the two-man teams reached the same conclusions, and the rest added side information which seemed to clarify and verify the news. It was discovered that the two sides in this fracas were drug cartels fighting a Chicago style gang war over territory infringements. Knowing this, Miller decided the team could ask more pertinent questions on their next trip to town. The next trip told the whole story, and the information was passed to EVEREST though our embassy. The San Pedro cartel was a government operated enterprise, and Senor Fernandez, the secretary of agriculture, was running the "farm." It was learned that Colonel Ortega inherited the enterprise during the coup. He had intended to destroy the operation, but when he saw the fantastic profitability, he put the profits to work building his fortune and his city. His national bank ran a money-laundering scheme which financed illegal syndicates all over the world, including an enormous illegal reelection campaign contribution to our previous president. As it turned out, this revelation added another ten years to his and his party chairman's prison terms. The bank also had a great stake in the oil industry of a South American neighbor. The bank funneled funds to special interest groups in the United States at attractive interest rates to pay for all sorts of nefarious schemes and political bribes. So like a spider's web, Ortega reached out in many illegal directions from the safety of the nation he ran. He had hoped to remain the silent partner, but now he was exposed as the big boss.

Receiving this intelligence, EVEREST thought it wise not to get involved in the internal problem of San Pedro when a third party might unknowingly help out. He decided to let the two cartels fight it out. Later when the dust settles, we can pick up the pieces. Normally a boycott of San Pedro would seem in order, but that would only alert Ortega.

On his return SPIRIT felt pleased with the outcome of operation CAUTIOUS HELP. Caution indeed had won the day and cost us almost nothing. He then turned his attention to possible outcomes to that fracas in the south and to possible actions which might be required—contingency planning. Later while relaxing, he did what he always did to relax; turn to the Lord. This time he thought Gods' plan works like this: *When you know God, everything comes together for good.*

CHAPTER 15

CSE CHALLENGE

With peace and tranquility at home, a secure and confident American could expect to raise moral and Christian-educated children, except for one thing—the illegal drug epidemic that had plagued the nation since the 1960's. Yes, a segment of the "flower children" was hooked and most high crimes and misdemeanors could be traced to drug addiction. Just as the prohibition amendment gave birth to organized crime in America, so drug trafficking created a giant and illegal power structure doing great harm to American culture, damaging it with the creation of a drug culture. It was clear the users would not quit as long as illicit drugs were readily available. Drug barons were murdering to protect their business. Because of America's addiction, profits were astronomical, and cartels were able to buy or intimidate governments and politicians and raise private armies to fight those who would try to cut off the supply. Drug smuggling felt no real threat from law enforcement. We seemed not to have the will to strongly oppose it. Law enforcement agencies were underfunded. People and local governments trying to be vigorous in their opposition were ruthlessly dealt with. High profile celebrities died of overdosing. They were only the visible tip of the iceberg. America tolerated the recreational drug use, which encouraged increased demand. Families were destroyed financially because once hooked at a low price, people had to pay the higher prices to feed their addictions. Driving a car drunk became DUI (diving under the influence) because drugs were a close second to alcohol as the cause of fatal accidents. All this because sensible Americans failed to insist on a crack-down on the drug menace. The ancient biblical term for this sin is *sorcery*, and God warns his children to stay clear.

* * *

Here are excerpts from a letter written by an Arizona State Senator explaining a law just signed by the Governor:

> Rancher Rob Krantz was murdered by the drug cartel on his ranch a month ago. I participated in a senate hearing two weeks ago on the border violence. Here are just some of the highlights from those who testified. The people who live within sixty to eighty miles of the Arizona/Mexico Border have for years been terrorized and have pleaded for help to stop the daily invasion of humans who cross their property. One rancher testified that 300 to 1200 people a day come across his ranch, vandalizing his property, stealing his vehicles and property, cutting down fences, and leaving trash. In the last two years he has found seventeen dead bodies and two Koran bibles.

> Another rancher testified that daily drugs are brought across his ranch in a military operation. A point man with a machine gun goes in front, half mile behind are the guards fully armed, half mile behind them are the drugs, behind the drugs half

mile are more guards. These people are violent and they will kill anyone who gets in the way. This was not the only rancher we heard that day that talked about the drug trains.

One man told of two illegals that came upon his property, one shot in the back and the other in the arm by the drug runners who had forced them to carry the drugs and then shot them. Daily they listen to gun fire during the night. It is not safe to leave his family alone on the ranch, and they can't leave the ranch for fear of nothing being left when they come back.

The border patrol is not on the border. They have set up sixty miles away with check points that do nothing to stop the invasion. They are not allowed to use force in stopping anyone who is entering. They run around chasing them. If they get their hands on them, then they can take them back across the border.

Federal prisons have over 35 percent illegals and 20 percent of Arizona prisons are filled with illegals. In the last few years 80 percent of our law enforcement that have been killed or wounded has been by an illegal.

...The Federal Government has refused for years to do anything to help the border states. We have been overrun, and once they are here, we have the burden of funding state services that they use. Education costs have been over a billion dollars. The healthcare cost billions of dollars. Our state is broke, $3.5 billion deficit, and we have many serious decisions to make. One is that we do not have the money to care for any who are not here legally. It has to stop.

…The Socialist who are in power in DC are angry because we dare try and do something, and that something the Socialists want us to do is just let them come. They want the transformation to continue.

Maybe it is too late to save America. Maybe we are not worthy of freedom anymore. But as an elected official, I must try to do what I can to protect our constitutional republic. Living in America is not a right just because you can walk across the border. Being an American is a responsibility, and it comes by respecting and upholding the constitution, the law of the land that says what you must do to be a citizen of this country. Freedom is not free."

* * *

The new president was angered by this injustice and the former administration's bullying of Arizona. He was determined to close our border and stop the drug running.

As a first step our courageous president decided that America must do all it can to dry up the market and end this tolerance of evil. He began a campaign to inform all Americans of the true character of our drug addiction in the hope he could shame the users and not only reduce demand but also discourage experimentation by teenagers. Over time teens became impressed with the stupidity of drug use and began ridiculing their peers. As it turned out nothing was more dreaded by a teenager than ridicule and ostracism. The president understood the grip of addiction made his program only moderately successful and proceeded to phase two of his plan--aggressive covert warfare to eliminate the drug lords. He wanted to announce to the world the fact that the drug barons lived under the threat of death at any time or place, but that would only alert them and make our job more difficult and costly in lives. So covert we must remain, and CSE once again would be a major player.

In the meantime a bill with teeth in it was introduced in congress establishing severe criminal penalties for drug offenders. Anyone at the top of US drug distribution chain and those heading delivery systems--thirty years in prison without possibility of parole. Pushers (anyone caught selling to individuals) were to be sentenced to ten years in prison without possibility of parole. Users refusing rehabilitation after being warned were to be sentenced to two years in rehab confinement. Users volunteering for rehab were to be confined until clean, free of charge. Second offenders were to be sentence to two years rehabilitative confinement. Those considered heads of drug cartels were sentenced to death in absentia—sentence to be carried out when captured or within weapons range. It was argued before the Supreme Court that we were at war with men known by the world as drug kingpins responsible for more deaths through murders, overdosing and gang killings than Osama bin Laden's attack on the World Trade Center and therefore could be executed without trial. Also, being a Christian nation, all rehabilitation programs included instruction in Christian doctrine for a clear understanding of the Christian's relationship with Christ. The bill passed the house and senate with little debate, signed by the president and determined to be constitutional by the Supreme Court with the provision that no one would be forced or coerced to adopt Christianity—all conversions must be left to the power in God's Word.

Armed with authority, it was now time to go to war in secret and CSE was ready. CLIMBER ordered all four task teams to assemble at MAGNOLIA to explain the president's directive and warn of its dangers.

"Gentlemen, oh boy, we've got a hot potato this time. The snakes we are after have the highest paid body guards in the world, and they have their own intelligence network. Cartels have had many years to perfect their security systems. If we make a mistake, it's sure to cost lives. These vermin are that good at their jobs. EVEREST has put a ten-million-dollar bounty on the head of one in particular, Pablo Bedoya, who heads the largest cartel. Hereafter, he will be referred to by his code name for the mission, SIDEWINDER. EVEREST feels the bounty on his head, along with witness protection, should draw out an informant or two. SPIRIT, you'll be interested to know the outcome of that quarrel in San Pedro. Ortega is dead, and SIDEWINDER has in effect taken over the country and placed a puppet president in place. Ortega gambled everything and went down fighting with most of his people. So, the president's decision to let them fight it out has narrowed the enemy down to SIDEWINDER and his gang. We've done what we can at this end of the chain, now it's time to chop off the head of this snake. In his own neighboring country the people love him because he comes across as kindly and generous giving large sums to needy charities and advertising the fact for his own glory. It certainly engendered loyalty but no treasure in heaven, right, SPIRIT?"

"It's in the Good Book, Sir."

"Right, but inwardly he is a ruthless killer, a deadly foe of those who would try to close down his business. In that regard our first order of business is determining how to get to him, how to get over, under, around or through his wall of security and returning unscathed. Satellite photography gives us some help with high definition pictures of suspected sites. In that poor country palatial estates are almost certainly paid for with drug money and therefore probable targets for drone strikes. We cannot arbitrarily hit these estates. We must have good reason to know our target is there. That's where CSE comes in. Our job is to snoop, and should our snooping provide an opportunity to engage our target, do so. In this kind of operation collateral damage is almost certain. I speak of SIDEWINDER's family. We must consider them as inheritors of the business should he die, and therefore legitimate collateral targets. It is known that his two sons occupy key positions in his organization. We also know his wife and daughter are well aware of the source of his wealth. So you see, we should have no qualms about taking out the entire evil family.

"SIDEWINDER owns a thirty-million-dollar diesel-motor yacht he named *My High,* and he spends a lot time aboard. It carries a helicopter. The vessel is 162 feet with a beam of thirty feet and a draft of eight feet. She has a range of four thousand nautical miles at seventeen knots. With it he could not only escape the country but escape the hemisphere. He's very proud of it and often holds conferences at sea. Only he knows where. The Italian builder told us the boat was, of course, guaranteed, and a factory maintenance man on call discovered the boat had been refitted with twin 40mm guns mounted fore and aft in innocent looking cocoons which could be jettisoned for action. The *My High* was designed to be operated by a crew of fourteen, the captain, first officer, communications officer, chef, cook and five stewards who double as gun crews, engineering officer with two assistants and a pilot. It also has luxury accommodations, with or without female companionship, for twelve guests. Quite a tub, what? We calculate it takes five thousand drug addicts just to supply its fuel to operate. By the way, the crew is augmented by two bodyguards when SIDEWINDER is aboard. Being who he is, wherever he is, everyone close to him risk becoming collateral damage. I say this because the day may come when we give that beautiful yacht the deep six together with all on board. So you see, we'll spare no expense to get this snake—of course in such a manner as she will simply disappear leaving the world to wonder. However, to do that, we first must find her. We do know she is not moored at any known marina. Somewhere along the coast it is hidden out of sight, well camouflaged, but we have ways.

"So our best cover is to create a civil war among the cartels in order to place plausible blame on others for our actions. EVEREST intends to make drug trafficking so mortally dangerous no one would consider the enterprise no matter how profitable. They must be convinced that profits would be as short term as their life spans—only weeks after being identified. Anyone siding with or protecting the drug czars would be considered collateral targets, so they'll soon learn to get out of the way!

"It boils down to this: US participation is to be secret and unilateral--that is governments would not be sure from where help was coming. The US will be happy to let them take credit for our success.

"So there's your mission. WIZARD, from here on you carry the ball."

"Aye, Sir." Then, turning to his team leaders the Admiral said, "We'll have a planning conference for all team leaders tomorrow morning at 1000 hours to discuss mission requirements and assignments. Until then give it some thought and come up with ideas for discussion. In case you're wondering, unlike previous missions, this job will take three teams working simultaneously and one in reserve just in case. And now SPIRIT will you lead us in prayer?"

"Yes Sir. Almighty God, we have had a terrible evil thrust upon us. It has invaded all walks of life in one way or another and morally weakened our beloved country. We ask your blessing in our fight to eliminate this drug evil. Speak to each of us as we prepare for the struggle before us so that we will do Your will. We trust in Your protection as well as Your inspiration for our actions. Help us, Lord, to snuff out this menace once and for all time in this country, for Yours is the Kingdom and the power and the glory forever. And everyone said, "Amen."

CHAPTER 16

TAKE UP THE GAUNTLET

There was high anticipation among the task teams. For three of the teams it was a long time since their last mission, and they were anxious to get back to work. They expected a challenge and began role-playing with each other to sharpen their wits. They tried not to overlook any sort of circumstance and tested their reaction to the dirtiest of tricks. So CLIMBER's orientation came as a welcome surprise--the surprise being the kind of mission and involving all four teams simultaneously.

The planning conference began promptly at 1000 hours. WIZARD had worked out the overall strategy and explained it to the team leaders, "Okay, so here's the plan for what we'll call OPERATION KINGPIN. We want to start a war—in-fighting among the drug cartels. When that gang war Chicago-style starts we will quietly lend a hand to be sure of reprisals. When we feel the time is right we'll hit the leaders. Sound simple? It won't be. Timing is critical. In that regard we hope the CIA will entice an informer to come forth. A ten-million-dollar bounty should bring someone out of the woodwork with information we can use. Our information is not exactly timely—nothing we can act on but generally useful. Until we know something definite, we must walk the thin line between caution and over-caution. SIDEWINDER is smart and at some point we expect him to call for a truce and peace talks which are likely to take place aboard the *My High* as an expression of the benefits of peaceful coexistence. However, once at sea he may decide to exterminate his opposition and send them to a watery grave. We understand he's done it before.

"Before we go any further, here are your assignments. HAMMER, your team will cause havoc in SIDEWINDER's home country, Tierra del Monte. TORNADO, you'll do the same in San Pedro. SPIRIT, you will find and sink the *My High*. MUSTANG, your team will be held in reserve to serve as a team replacement or to provide individual replacements if needed. Now that you know your assignments, I want HAMMER and TORNADO, as teams with similar missions, to brainstorm together for the next forty-eight hours to take advantage of each other's ideas. We'll then reconvene and review the situation. I expect by then we'll have more information. SPIRIT, please remain with me. This meeting is adjourned."

WIZARD then reached into his brief case and produced a US Coast Guard document and a photograph of what appeared to be a yacht in the style popular on the 1920s. It didn't appear to be a threat of any kind. WIZARD pushed the document and photo toward SPIRIT without saying a word. SPIRIT first notice the Top Secret classification and let out a low whistle. He picked up the photo and studied it.

"It looks like an antique."

"She--"

"Sir?"

"She. You come from a navy family, you should know enough to refer to a ship as a she. They call her *Miss Liberty*. None of her targets have lived to tell about her. She's that secret. We requisitioned this innocent appearing civilian vessel to search the coast. In fact, she is equipped with all the latest electronic marvels and concealed armament including two torpedo tubes. Unlike the PT boats of WWII, the tubes are not on the deck, but instead this craft has internal tubes in the bow just under the water line, like a submarine. But this boat can't dive. To add to the deception, it looks like an antique, but it is truly a high-speed patrol craft which can easily outrun any known yacht. You'll carry four torpedoes of the homing type—hard to miss your target. These fish are somewhat smaller and ten times more powerful than our WWII torpedoes. One hit and the *My High* is history. It may take a long time to find your target and many patrols, so to avoid being sighted, you will patrol only at night under blackout. Your sophisticated radar will be your eyes. *My High* also has eyes, so monitor your radar detector closely. If they detect you, you'll also know their location. Radar in hiding can be detected and pinpointed as to location, so while in hiding the vessel should emit no heat or electronic waves if it is to stay undetected. However, at sea all its electronic protection devices will be in use. In this situation engagement will require naval battle maneuvering. Your innocent and outdated vessel is in fact a deadly patrol torpedo boat."

SPIRIT was intrigued by the capabilities of the vessel but wondered, "Am I supposed to skipper this craft?"

"Yes, but you and your team will go to school for a two-week crash course by the coast guard and they insisted on providing you with an advisor on your mission. They are rather fond of this craft, so he was a condition to letting us borrow it."

"I can use a nautical education; someday my wife may buy me a yacht. She'll be impressed by what I know."

"One thing you may not know is armor warfare is much like naval warfare. You have much the same freedom of maneuver. Your instincts as a tanker will serve you well at sea, where there is no restriction of terrain to hamper your movement."

"Now that you mention it I recall an instructor at the Armor School making that comparison in reverse."

WIZARD the admiral thought a moment and said, "After this experience you may want to transfer to the navy."

"I don't know. If my tank breaks down, I can walk a lot farther than I can swim."

WIZARD picked up the photo and glanced at it momentarily before placing it back in his briefcase. "Getting back to naval tactics, here's one other item that should prove useful. This craft is equipped with a smoke generator in case you should want to disappear. The coast guard will teach you its tactical use. You will patrol searching for the *My High*, but when you find her, head for the open sea and wait for the code word GALAXY from one of our teams ashore, which indicates she's about to put to sea with SIDEWINDER aboard. Should you not get the code word and sight the *My High* on radar and the helicopter is aboard along with passengers, sink her. He has more than once used these conferences at sea to kill and dispose of the bodies in shark infested waters. Because of the curvature of the earth, one cannot see from the surface a craft with the naked eye beyond twenty miles on a clear day. These conferences are held far from coastal surveillance--one or two hundred miles out. It is there you must sink her. Her disappearance without a trace should strike fear into the remainder of the cartel personnel--that and the activity of our teams ashore. In peacetime the coast guard operates under the control of the Department of the Treasury, but in wartime it is under the Department of Defense. Your Coast Guard advisor will know only that you are in command. You must emphasize to him that he has no say in your mission and that his only interest is the safety of the vessel. Neither he nor the Coast Guard is aware of your target or the existence of CSE."

Two days later WIZARD discussed the mission with the assembled teams, "Okay, refresh my memory, how many of you are qualified snipers?" Two men in each team raised their hands. "Good, you in teams HAMMER and TORNADO will be equipped with a new large caliber sniper rifle with a powerful telescopic sight. It has an effective range of one mile. Get familiar with it and practice at maximum range with human-sized targets. It fires three types of ammo--ball, armor-piercing, and an explosive round with slightly shorter range that will detonate explosives and ignite fuel.

"Now for the matter of your entry into the country, both embassies are overstaffed, so the team leaders and two others will enter each country under diplomatic immunity and the others as tourist on a different flight. Embassies are closely watched, so as you three enter, another three will depart for home so it will appear you are replacements to the embassy. As diplomats your baggage cannot be searched. Your disassembled rifles will be in your baggage. Once in country your team will reassemble and carry out your mission. The sniper rifle with its extraordinary range is a terror weapon. Its victim and anyone with him will probably not be alerted by the sound of a shot from such a distance, and it will be relatively easy for you to disappear. Your only real problem will be positive identification of your target. The military attaché has photos and will fill you in on known cartel people. Another thing: we're not looking for something extreme to really rile the other gang like the Saint Valentine's Day massacre. That might start a no quarter war that would end with one powerful drug lord and the continual flow of merchandise into the United States. We want an action that could logically lead to a cease fire and peace talks aboard the *My High*. We are counting on SIDEWINDER's pride in the vessel and his habit of conducting conferences on board. In other words we want to give SPIRIT a juicy target--all eggs in one basket so to speak."

It was time for Team SPIRIT to go to school. All instruction took place aboard the *Miss Liberty* and covered seamanship, ordnance, navigation, electronics, search and rescue, and classic PT boat tactics. SPIRIT assigned two of his team members to each specialized subject, but all took the training to gain a working knowledge of all areas of duty on board in an emergency. In two weeks *Miss Liberty* had her crew and put to sea. A few days prior to her sailing teams HAMMER and TORNADO were deployed and began their mischief. What little information provided by the embassy was enough to stir things up. Had they known more it might have started a situation that would become unmanageable. A hornet sting would have been too irritating. A flea bite would be enough.

Cartel members were mysteriously dropped in their tracks by a weapon their companions could not locate. Fuel tanks supplying electricity generators providing power to isolated but palatial estates were blown up by explosive ammunition from the long-reach rifles. Although a silencer was provided it couldn't completely silence such a large caliber weapon, so in urban areas, where the muffled report could be heard, a deception plan imitated the sound and would continue until positively identified as other than a rifle shot.

As it worked out SIDEWINDER naturally knew more about the opposing cartel that we did and ordered more effective retaliation forcing the cartels into peace negotiations. He set the time and the expected place of their conference.

SPIRIT studied the charts of the rugged coastline and had not yet located the *My High*. He searched for an inlet large enough to conceal a 162-foot vessel with an eight-foot draft and remain hidden even from an air search. It would have to be a place deep enough where the vessel could safely ride out a low tide. SIDEWINDER being immensely rich, cost was no concern. He could do what seemed impossible in constructing a hiding place on a portion of the seacoast he already owned. The rugged cliffs were higher than the mast of the *My High*. Radar scans of a hundred miles of coastline disclosed nothing on three patrols. Comparisons of photos taken of likely locations showed nothing suspicious. SPIRIT encoded a message to WIZARD requesting an over flight with infrared photography. They continued patrolling while they awaited an answer. Twenty hours later the answer came:

SIDEWINDER did his best to shield *My High* from infrared detection. Photos showed none of the usual details, but he couldn't shield the shield. Photos revealed a pale rectangular image that wasn't there on five year old photos of the area. Photo attached. We have learned cartel conference called for three days hence. Good hunting—WD.

That night the MISS LIBERTY sailed to a position opposite the spot indicated and at dawn they cruised slowly passed it. SPIRIT checked the terrain features and located the exact spot on the photo. There seemed to be nothing there. If the *My High* was there, the camouflage was masterful. The rocky face of the cliff appeared real. A second look at his chart revealed a narrow inlet he hadn't before considered. It seemed too tight a fit for a vessel that size. He decided to send in a scuba team for a closer underwater look. Under cover of a riotous party on board the *Miss Liberty* he dropped the three-man team over the seaward side and sailed on southward to return in two hours to pick them up.

Upon their return the divers reported they found the *My High* in what at first appeared to be a natural cavern, except the sixty-foot ceiling was man-made. The water was 20 feet deep. A steel stairway inside led to the top of the bluff. The divers never left the water and were not seen but observed the crew onboard making preparations to sail. Having accomplished their mission they returned to the pick-up line and were retrieved by the moving *Miss Liberty* in frogman fashion. They described the gate to the cavern as a steel framed replica of the stone face of the bluff and added, "...a very expensive hiding place for a very expensive yacht."

Now there was nothing to do but sail out of sight to the near limit of their radar and watch and wait for the snake to come out of his hole. In the meantime SPIRIT called the team together to explain his plan, "Here is what we intend to do. When we see her on the radar, we'll maneuver to trail her out of sight using radar until she is well out to sea, eighty to hundred nautical miles. Then at full speed a thousand yards off her port side, we lay a smoke screen until we are well ahead of her. Then we'll turn hard to port behind our screen and swing back 180 degrees and let her have one torpedo using radar with another ready after we break through the smoke screen, just in case. One should do the job because these torpedoes are ten times more powerful than the WWII types which were designed to blow a hole in the ship. Ours are designed to blow the vessel out of the water."

Two nights later the crafty SIDEWINDER put to sea early. The announced day and time served as a deception. Code word GALAXY was never received. Radar showed the departure of the *My High* in the darkness just before dawn. SPIRIT ordered a wide swing to come in behind her before dawn, well out of sight. Four hours of tracking took them eighty-six nautical miles to sea. The ocean surface was relatively smooth, ideal for the fast maneuver he planned. He ordered full speed. As they drew within sight of the *My High*, they moved to about a thousand yards to her port and began laying their smoke screen. SPIRIT knew he had alerted SIDEWINDER, but at the speed of 35 knots he would be on him before he could evade contact. All he had time to do was to uncover his 40mm guns. He wouldn't know where along the smoke screen the *Miss Liberty* would appear even if he suspected the maneuver. Then it would be too late. As they circled, SPIRIT's radar showed the *My High* to be in perfect position for attack. SPIRIT ordered, "Stand by for torpedo attack! Open outer doors!"

The reply came, "Number one ready!" Then, "Number two ready!"

"Stand by." Then, with *Miss Liberty* still behind her smoke screen, SPIRIT relying on radar and the homing torpedo ordered, "Fire one!"

"One away!" came the reply. SPIRIT checked his watch for the running time and as they broke through the screen, he looked up and watched the *My High* disappear in an enormous explosion. The shock wave rocked the *Miss Liberty.*

An astonished S42 uttered, "They didn't have a chance."

To which SPIRIT answered, "They weren't meant to."

He then encoded a short success message to WIZARD,

My High blown sky high, no survivors--ST

Then over the intercom he spoke to his team, "There can be no peaceful coexistence with evil."

CHAPTER 17

END OF THE BEGINNING

The president was elated at the news, but he couldn't shake the feeling that the drug war was just beginning and OPERATION KINGPIN was a good start and should make events to come somewhat more manageable. The law and penalties were in place. An information campaign made every man, woman and child aware of the drug evil. It would take a concerted effort by law enforcement at all levels to clean up America. As the country's appetite dried up, the drug prices would go down. That together with the harsh penalties would discourage would-be dealers from taking the risk. It just wasn't worth it.

Everything in the president's plan to heal America was designed to target one evil—*greed*. This became so apparent to the people that in every endeavor people paused to asked themselves, "Is this reasonable or am I being greedy?" America learned that money was not the root of all evil. It was the *love of money* that was evil. The culture of greed which brought us so close to destruction was dying, but understanding human nature, the president did all he could to imbed a new commandment in America's conscience. "Thou shall not be greedy." The litmus test for every business transaction was "will this hurt anybody." Breaking faith with loyal senior employees by firing them and replacing them with low-entry-wage people to improve the bottom line became a crime punishable by a stiff fine calculated to erase the amount of money saved by such action. He repeated many times during his media chats that nothing is more important than the value and dignity of a single human soul. The Bible tells us to love one another as we love ourselves. America must be constantly reminded to do unto others as you would have them do unto you—the golden rule set forth in the Holy Scriptures.

Yes, America had been born again; but like raising a young child, repetition is the key to learning, and once a lesson is learned, it must be passed on to generation after generation without alteration. God's truth is truth for all time, but because we are human we are blind to this reality. To the growing child God's truth has the most powerful impact when it comes from all quarters of life, home, church, classroom and occupation. Whatever the situation, truth is that which agrees with the word of God. When in doubt, stop and ask yourself, *What would Jesus do?* Perfection is in the supreme wisdom of God's Word—there is no better idea.

In a conversation with Bill Bowman, I myself had to be reminded by his free admission that, spiritually speaking, he was most vulnerable to Satan's attacks when he neglected reading his Bible daily. Application of God's Word in daily life situations requires not only a knowledge of His Word but also frequent reminders to keep us from straying like lost sheep. We must understand that the Good Shepherd is our only protection from the folly of man. Nothing dies that is remembered.

On April 30, 1802 Thomas Jefferson wrote, "Religion, morality, and knowledge being necessary to good government and the happiness of mankind, (of this) schools and the means of education shall forever be encouraged."

As President, Thomas Jefferson created chaplains in Congress and the armed forces, but when signing the Articles of War he earnestly recommended to all officers and soldiers, diligently to attend divine services."

* * *

During one of his chats to the people our new president said, "It is the duty of the leaders of the governments at all levels of a Christian nation to protect and preserve the morals of its citizens. That is why we have laws to punish offenders. It follows that voting citizens should be cautious and not hand over power to atheists, anarchist, or to a person holding beliefs other than Christian. If a president lied about his qualifications for office he must be impeached. A candidate who lies simple cannot be trusted to lead a moral country. Yes, we believe in freedom of religion and we are tolerate others, but if we are to remain strong we must remain united in language and religion because divided we fall. Before a Muslim, Hindu or a Buddhist can become a naturalized citizen all must swear allegiance to our God-given Constitution; if not they are aliens and not entitled to the privileges of a citizen offered by the federal, state or local governments.

"Much of what I have said applies to our war on drugs. In this war every citizen is a soldier and expected to do their duty. Every illegal drug transaction observed must be reported. Identities of reporting citizens will be kept confidential. Cell phones have made reporting easy; just call 911 and the police will take over from there.

"Citizens, we are a team. As team players we must all do our part if we are to win. Let us all work to enjoy the home of the bravest enough to report evil, and earn God's blessing. Until next time, goodnight my friends."

* * *

The president's chats were always a popular subject of conversation and public confidence was high. People compared him to another president who saved a divided union, Abraham Lincoln. High praise indeed and well deserved.

Toni switched off the TV and smiled at Bill; both very much impressed with the president's chat. Toni spoke first, "Oh honey, do we have a president or what? Wow, he tells it like it is, a true patriot doing what is right and not caring if he is reelected or not."

"He doesn't have to worry about reelection, he'll be drafted. The people won't let him quit after only one term. After what he's accomplished in one term his reelection will be a landslide."

"If it isn't a sure thing the voters will be stupid and ungrateful. What he has accomplished makes me proud to be an American. What more can he do?"

Bill replied, "How high is up? He's shown the new generation what democracy means. Frankly, I'm excited when I think he'll have another term to be sure his measures in place are functioning smoothly. Americans must be sleeping well these nights."

Giving Bill an alluring look, Toni said seductively, "Who wants to sleep? Let's go to bed my love."

"Like the president, you lay it all on the line, don't you."

"Lover, when opportunity knocks… open the door."

Looking Toni up and down, Bill said, "I'd be a fool not to."

A new day had dawned, and MUSTANG, who was left out of OPERATION KINGPIN was next up. Awaiting the next alert, all teams were occupied with drug war concerns and assembling all the information available. All of SIDEWINDER's fields were burned and labs destroyed, but there remained a slow trickle of drugs which threatened to grow as small operators saw a chance to grab a bigger piece of the pie. So the drug war continues. A rejuvenated Border Patrol worked the north side of the border with the help of the National Guard, but it became apparent that CSE needed to conduct clandestine operations south of the border to discourage the infiltrators while government negotiations continued. If agreement wasn't reached soon, a boycott of products made south of the border would begin. Corporations in the states were warned to have plans ready to manufacture items now made or assembled there. All we ask is that Mexico have the same objectives and to be as aggressive in the drug war as we.

EVEREST considered it might be that Mexico needs American industry to make staying in country more attractive with additional jobs. At any rate as a separate operation the crossing of drug traffic must be stopped and CSE was to lend a hand. Team MUSTANG will pinpoint the location of drug operation targets for appropriate strikes and to eliminate key smugglers when the evidence and opportunity presented itself.

Meanwhile, *Miss Liberty* went back to work. Coast Guard interdiction of suspected drug carrying vessels was stepped up with the assistance of the navy. Secret Service agents were assigned to public and private airfields to inspect incoming aircraft. Radar tracked private planes crossing the border to their landing sites where roving SWAT teams waited to search. Now it depended on everybody doing their jobs and doing them well.

After cleaning our own house, the next item on the president's agenda for recovery was for America not to be led into a one world government by foreign leaders who do not share our beliefs. Truly, without the influence, expense, and coercion from the United Nations, America is once again an independent, sovereign nation in control of her own destiny and a player in world affairs, but on her own terms and under God's guidance.

CHAPTER 18

THREE YEARS LATER

I t was not a quick war. War never is. Battles yes, but the war goes on, and as planned, inexpensive in material and lives. WIZARD was proud of CSE's impressive record in the war against evil tyrants; however, he was tired, and retirement age was upon him. As CSE chief of staff, he had worked for five chairmen of the joint chiefs. Now a sixth was to assume the code name CLIMBER. This brought up the question of continuity. EVEREST, whose election to a second term had been certain, wanted experience to maintain efficient operations. The loss of his two top men was disturbing, and he asked the outgoing CLIMBER for his recommendation to replace WIZARD.

Another change came as a surprise to me. In an unusual manner I was informed that my code name was to be changed from SCOOP to MULEY. I learned that my friend and colleague Brigadier General Betancourt had decided to retire and that I was to assume his rank and position as the army's historian.

Court had given me no inkling of his plan to retire, and the subject of his eventual replacement never came up. This event reversed our positions. As a civilian, he would write for public consumption and I would take care of the top secret shop. So it was agreed that I would immediately assume my new duty, with General Betancourt looking over my shoulder until his request for retirement was approved. My first duty was to prepare the secret conference room for a meeting with EVEREST, CLIMBER, and WIZARD the following day, the subject being the successor to WIZARD.

As the meeting convened, EVEREST offered three names for consideration, an Admiral and two Generals--one army and one marine. CLIMBER, out of courtesy to EVEREST, examined the records of the three. All seemed qualified. Then he looked up at WIZARD, who nodded. CLIMBER turned to the President and explained, "WIZARD and I anticipated the need for his eventual replacement. We agreed some time ago that from the experience and security standpoints, it would be desirable to appoint someone from in house."

EVEREST questioned, "Who, there's no one with the rank to take over?"

"That's a technicality that can be easily overcome. What is important is hands-on experience, and we have your man."

"Who?"

"Our best team leader, SPIRIT, he's your man."

"A Lieutenant Colonel?" EVEREST paused in thought, then, "Someone working so close to me should be a General."

CLIMBER thought for a moment and added, "SPIRIT is a highly decorated officer and commands the love and respect of everyone in CSE."

"Love?"

"Yes, Sir, there's not a man in CSE who wouldn't lay down his life for him. You may not know it, but he is the holder of the Distinguished Service Cross and the Medal of Honor. You may also be interested to know that he was requested by the men to be their unofficial chaplain. He is a fine leader, the best we have. Both WIZARD and I have the highest confidence in his ability. This is the job he has been groomed for. We feel you couldn't make a better choice."

"It's a stupid man that doesn't take the advice of experts. Okay, I'll award him the Legion of Merit and fly over Colonel and promote SPIRIT to Brigadier General."

CLIMBER's reply came as a request, "Major General...Sir?"

"Okay, have it your way. That's the least I can do for the magnificent service he has rendered our country."

Returning to MAGNOLIA, CLIMBER and WIZARD called an extraordinary conference of all four teams to take place as soon as the team on leave arrived. Meanwhile, it was decided that, all teams being equal, they should be led by the same rank, Lieutenant Colonel, and no team member would be below the rank of Captain. Thereto, all NCOs would be promoted. After all, they were exceptional men fighting a dangerous shadow war for their country. Prior to the conference SPIRIT was summoned to WIZARD's office. Upon arrival SPIRIT, being a highly trained observer, noticed the Admiral's flag behind the desk had changed color from blue to red and showed only two stars, prompting SPIRIT to ask, "Sir, what happened to the third star on your flag?"

"Are you color blind? That's not my flag, that's yours."

"What?"

"This is your office."

"Is this a joke?"

What follows is his last word as WIZARD. "A week from today I'll be a civilian. Effective as of this moment, you my friend are WIZARD." He then reached into his pocket and retrieved the two star insignia of rank and walked to Major General Hunter William Bowman to pin the stars to his collar. Then breaking his own rule that all in Magnolia be called by their code names, he said, "I could not be prouder Bill. CSE has been the longest and best duty assignment of my career. I've known a lot of fine officers and men in my life, but you, my friend have been the best. I leave

CSE in good hands." He paused. His eyes glazed, and he finally said, "You who always say the right thing at the right time have nothing to say?" Bill hesitated and then,

"I'm stunned, it's not every day a man becomes a Major General, especially when he didn't expect it. I never dreamed I...I know you had a hand in my jumping three grades. Thank you. I suppose in time I'll recover from the shock, but I don't know how long it will take."

"Well it better be soon because, as WIZARD, you have a task to perform tomorrow. Here's the plan. At the conference I'll open by announcing my retirement. You will be just outside the door out of sight. Then in a few words I'll introduce the new WIZARD. When I ask you to step forward, you come in, walk down the aisle, and take the platform. When things quiet down, we will call each team to the platform one at a time and present them with their new insignia of rank. When we're through, there won't be an NCO in the house. With that done the next order of business is who will be the new SPIRIT?"

"S42, my right-hand-man. Will he be surprised, Captain to Lieutenant Colonel in one jump--he and HAMMER both. As a Second Lieutenant in Korea Hammer was my Platoon Sergeant. I recruited him into this business.

"Yes I remember. Now let's take those stars off your collar. We don't want to give the show away. Put them back on tomorrow just before the conference ceremony."

The next morning the conference room buzzed with questions and conjecture. Then someone commanded, *"Atten-chut!"*

The Admiral entered the room and strode directly to the platform. "At ease. Take seats gentlemen. I've called you all together to announce my retirement from the navy." There was a groan of surprise and regret from the men to which he responded, "Thank you, gentlemen, but after thirty-six years of active service I've decided to call it a career. My greatest pleasure was serving with you gentlemen. Outside the military there is a different world, one of eroded values. I thank God for a commander in chief doing his best to bring those values back in line with ours and our founding fathers. I appreciate the privilege of serving my country in the company of courageous men and women of honesty and integrity. I know I'll miss you all. Now I have an idea you must have some small interest in my replacement. He wasn't hard to find. So let me now introduce your new WIZARD. Will you come forward please? Everyone turned to look back down the aisle. WIZARD marched briskly to the platform to the shouts and cheers of the men, the two stars shining brightly on his collar. The applause continued for over a minute until WIZARD raised his hands to quiet them down.

"Thank you ... thank you very much." A second wave of applause erupted. "Alright, enough already." The men were laughing as the applause finally ended. "Thanks again. I can't tell you how much that reception means to me. I must say I had no forewarning of this giant vault upward in grade. I'm more than a little astonished at the somewhat dizzying event. I'm told that I have replaced WIZARD. I want to say here and now that can't be done, but I'll do my best." The men agreed with a rousing round of applause as he continued. Then turning to the Admiral he said, "Some time ago I told you we, to a man, would regret you leaving CSE, and that's true. But speaking for us all, we wish you a long, happy, and healthy retirement. And by the way, we'd all be interested in your memoirs." At this there was another round of applause. Then WIZARD added, "But that part concerning CSE will have to be classified. Yes, I was delighted by the promotion, but now as my first act as WIZARD, it gives me great pleasure to spring a surprise on you, my friends. A grateful EVEREST has proudly taken another extraordinary step in the history of CSE, but first I want to announce the appointment of the new leader of Team SPIRIT. I'd like the entire team to stand and remain standing after I call his name. S42, you are now SPIRIT."

After the applause, he said, "First EVEREST promotes each team leader to Lieutenant Colonel." Again cheers echoed throughout MAGNOLIA.

"Second he also stated that no one in CSE will carry a rank below Captain. You who already are Captains are promoted to Major. I would like to be the first to congratulate you Non Commissioned Officers on your commissioning to Captain. The room once again erupted in cheers and applause.

"And now with the assistance of the Admiral we will present individually your new insignia of rank. Starting with Team SPIRIT already standing, file up to the platform and receive our heartiest congratulations and your new commissions."

It had been a long and eventful day for Bill, and he missed going home to his lover; however, she had gone to Tierra Blanca on business and a short visit to her parents. He delayed departure from MAGNOLIA, and arrived late in Atlanta. It had been three days since he had seen her. With no mission directive forthcoming, he'd asked for a week off, expecting Toni's imminent return. When he drove into the condo's basement garage, he saw Toni's car back from the airport. She was home. Quickly he decided to change into uniform there in the basement. He thought, *Won't she be surprised?* Toni had never ever seen Bill in uniform. It will be the first time he would make love as a major general. He mused, N*ow there's a silly thought.* He decided not to use his key and just ring the bell so she would open the door and behold a Major General. He did and she did. Toni took one look and never having seen Bill in uniform said playfully, "Bill's not home." Then she shut the door in his face, leaving Bill standing momentarily before opening the door once more and saying, "What's this? You really know how to bowl a girl over."

"My dear you are now the lady of a major general."

"You told me only a month ago your rank was lieutenant colonel. That's a big jump. Do you have a new job? "

"Same old stand, but now I'm the boss. Still, that's all I can say."

"Wow, I'm going to be awake half the night in bed with a Major General. That puts a new light on our love making."

"Are my stars that bright?"

"They dazzle me. No kidding, I'm so proud of you, love."

"Awe honey, no General has a more beautiful wife and lover."

"I like that last part, come here." Their lingering kiss was the beginning of another of many magical evenings as man and wife.

The years passed quickly, as they do when you are busy, and CSE remained active. Two more presidents found CSE a useful tool, and America grew stronger and more righteous. Prosperity brought happy results, a dwindling prison population and a unity of purpose no tyrant dared to oppose. Everyone who wanted a job had one. The lack of corporate greed had the effect of increasing job availability. Human dignity was restored. Citizens felt a security they hadn't known before. Americans realized that taking their freedoms for granted would be a grave error, leaving them open to attacks from within and without. They finally understood they must work for freedom responsibly each and every day.

As CSE historian, I decided since he was near retirement, to set apart Bill Bowman's remarkable service to his country by writing his story in two books, *Code Name: WILLIAM TELL* and *Code Name: SPIRIT*. Classified top secret and of course unpublished, I gave the manuscripts to the president to read. The president being new to the office, the books served to familiarize him with the distinguished but dark history of CSE and Bill Bowman, also known as WIZARD, in particular. I'll never forget the president's reaction to the books, "This man's career makes mine look puny. What he has done in total is amazing. He deserved the Medal of Honor several times for the services he has rendered. Has anyone been awarded the CMH twice?"

"No Sir, not one."

"Then I intend to make history. In secret, of course. I'll have CLIMBER set up a quiet ceremony in your conference room at MAGNOLIA."

"Well deserved Sir."

"Yes, the world has turned over many times since the creation of this remarkable band of men, and lately there has been little need for their services. I don't want to be too hasty in this, but if all goes well, we may be able to declassify CSE by the end of my term. What do you think?"

"Sir, I am the historian and I'd be delighted with the go-ahead to publish my books. But you should be asking CLIMBER and WIZARD that question. But, since you ask, I think you're right. Let's not be too hasty. Time will tell."

Yes, there was another extraordinary event in CSE's history. This president of the United States was the first visitor to MAGNOLIA. He marveled at the entry procedure as they proceeded through the 120 yard concrete reinforced tunnel to the elevator where he and CLIMBER were asked electronically for their code names and then were admitted. This was a president's first meeting with all the courageous men of CSE. A reception line was formed, and then EVEREST said, "It is my profound privilege to shake the hand of each of you."

Thereafter a special ceremony was held. Then EVEREST's opening remarks explained why this ceremony and all activities of CSE, was classified TOP SECRET, "I am told that there is no precedent for what I am about to do. Even so, I feel extraordinary recognition is most deserving of a career so remarkable as to not have been equaled in our nation's history, a career that has saved perhaps millions of innocent lives; an extraordinary recognition of an extraordinary career of an extraordinary man--in particular his career in the shadows of secrecy. One day when the story of CSE is told, you will all enjoy the fame you so richly deserve. But I could not let pass the opportunity to recognize privately the devotion to duty of your chief of staff, WIZARD, aka Major General Hunter William Bowman, to whom I now award the Congressional Medal of Honor with Oak Leaf Cluster with the thanks of a grateful nation." Cheers and applause erupted for their much loved and respected leader. EVEREST continued, "The details in his citation are classified top secret to be made public upon declassification of CSE. So if WIZARD will step forward it will be my privilege to place the Medal of Honor

142 COLONEL DON WILSON

142 | COLONEL DON WILSON

142 — COLONEL DON WILSON

142 COLONEL DON WILSON

142 COLONEL DON WILSON

around your neck." As he fastened the clasp behind his neck, EVEREST whispered, "Bill, I've never had a happier duty. I wish I could shout it to the world."

"Thank you Mister President."

So ended thirty years of extraordinary and distinguished service to his country. A man code named WILLIAM TELL, SPIRIT, and then WIZARD once again became Hunter William Bowman, now major general, US Army retired. Both he and Toni remain active in their church and live peacefully somewhere in quiet anonymity at his request. By my reckoning, he and Toni recently celebrated their forty-sixth wedding anniversary.

This book is the result of the declassification of CSE. I am proud and privileged to make public the remarkable story of these hitherto hidden heroes and their shadowy world of secret service to our nation. Your appreciation and thanks are worth more than all the medals and promotions we in CSE received. Never forget them. They didn't just serve. Their deeds made them heroes.

WARNING

Except for authentic quotations, this story is fiction. I've tried to paint a picture of what I believe we should have done to save our nation. Over the years the bright hope that was America faded because the majority of our people have drifted into paganism. They believed the false prophets we call the enlightened ones, who thought they had a better idea than our Creator. That wonderful vision of our Founding Fathers has disappeared into the fog of disbelief and ignorance. Generations have been deprived of all knowledge of the Creator of the universe. Some even see God as the villain instead of their Savior. We have legalized sin to ease our conscience without reference to the infallible Bible.

What's happening?

That's the question we should all be asking ourselves. Some know the answer in part, and others haven't a clue because they were born in this generation of selfishness, misinformation, and media blindness. The Reverend Billy Graham sums up what has happened over the past generation in this prayer:

Heavenly Father, we come before you today to ask your forgiveness and to seek your direction and guidance. We know Your Word says, "Woe to those who call evil good," but that's exactly what we've done. We have lost our spiritual equilibrium and reversed our values. We have exploited the poor and called it the lottery. We have rewarded laziness and called it welfare. We have killed the unborn and called it choice. We have shot abortionists and called it justifiable. We have neglected to discipline our children and called it self-esteem. We have abused power and called it politics. We have coveted our neighbor's possessions and called it ambition. We have polluted the air with profanity and pornography and called it freedom of expression. We have ridiculed the time-honored values of our forefathers and called it enlightenment. Search us, Oh God, and know our hearts today; cleanse us from every sin and Set us free. *Amen!*

Commentator **Paul Harvey** featured this prayer on his radio program, *'The Rest of the Story'* and received the largest response of any program he has ever aired.

My friends, if you don't stand for something, you'll fall for anything. The bigger the lie, the more likely you'll believe it. Isn't it strange that we've known that for a long time, but when it happened we didn't recognize it. This nation is living a monstrous lie because we have forgotten who we are, how we got here, and where we should be going. Our clergy should be standing strong and echoing Billy Graham's indictment. They should be shaming loud and often an education system which prohibits the mention of almighty God in the classroom.

God's Word continues to warn us today. History repeats itself. You've no doubt heard that before. The science of archeology supports the fact that the Bible is an accurate history of its time.

The prophets of the Old Testament were God's messengers to a stiff necked people like us. Bible prophecy--and there are hundreds--has predicted ahead of time events that took their place in history. Yes, there are prophecies that are yet to be fulfilled, but with a perfect record how can they not be believed? The warnings of old and their fulfillment are warnings for today. Allow me an example, Proverbs 3:3-7 says,

> Let not mercy and truth forsake you; bind them around your neck, write them on the tablet of your heart, and so find favor and high esteem in the sight of God and man. Trust in the Lord with all of your heart, and lean not on your own understanding; in all your ways acknowledge Him; and He shall *direct* your paths. Do not be wise in your own eyes; fear the Lord and depart from evil.

What King Solomon, who wrote many of the proverbs, is telling us is that we must learn the Bible in order to know God and His plan for living. He at a glance sees all--past, present and future. He has omniscience, an ability no human has. We view the passing parade through a knothole in the fence. We cannot see the beginning and the end, but God can. His guidance is infallible. Follow it and have a happy and secure life. He offers hope, the secret of life, and He keeps his promises. For those who believe in Him, He promises a heavenly destination. Your friends can't see an hour ahead so don't rely on their word over the supreme wisdom of God. The very purpose of life is to glorify God.

I heard a story the other day that tells it all. A man arrived at heaven's gate and was greeted by Saint Peter. He was told to explain why he should be admitted to heaven, and he would be awarded points for every reason. It would take hundred points to enter. The man began, "I attended church every Sunday."

"Okay,..." Saint Peter replied, "...that's 2 points."

"Only 2? I've been faithful to my marriage vows."

"Alright, that's good for 1 point."

"Only 1 point? I don't swear, smoke or drink."

"Good, that's another point."

"One point? At this rate the only way I'll get to heaven is by the grace of God."

"Very good, Ninety-six points. Welcome to the Kingdom of God."

This book is a fictional adventure story housing answers to what needs to be done to restore the *intent* of our Founding Fathers when, with God's guidance, they wrote our Constitution. The Ten Commandments applied to government. Had we remained God's people, we would not have brought upon ourselves the dire consequences we face today. The Holy Bible specifies the way to a happy life; however, we stopped reading it, and now we are paying the penalty for our paganism.

What did God do when sinners repeatedly failed to repent? He gave them over to depravity. He said in effect, "I'll have nothing to do with you until your life gets so horrendous that you turn back to Me and pray for my forgiveness." The stubborn children of Israel suffered severe consequences. Over the years Syria, Babylon and Rome not only conquered Israel but destroyed Jerusalem, the temple, and scattered their people. Even though these nations were pagan, God used them to punish Israel in the hope that she would come back to Him for salvation. Sound familiar?

The Holy Scriptures are filled with prophesies, 100 percent of which have come true in their time. In our time there is no mention of America, because God has left us to our sins. The end is near. There will be no recent history as described in this book. We will not recover our greatness. God said, "Many will be called, but few will answer." But those who do answer will be saved from the coming tribulation and reside with Him in glory. We call it The Rapture. We will ascend to heaven just as Jesus did and leave the pagans behind to face the tribulation of the Antichrist and Armageddon. Understand we are all sinners. No Christian can claim he or she is not a sinner. Having asked His forgiveness and given God *all* our heart, mind, and strength, we are saved by His grace. Jesus took all our sins to hell with him, becoming sin Himself to save you. Three days later He rose from the tomb. That sacrifice freed the Christian from condemnation. God is love. He doesn't expect us to be perfect, but we must make the attempt. Remember, "Good deeds are but filthy rags without faith." As a Christian myself, it is my duty to look to my fellow man, sinner or saint, and point the way. When you read the Bible God will do the saving.

Metal must be refined to rid it of impurities. A Christian education does that for us. A study of the world's all-time best seller puts you high on the list of the wise and knowledgeable. If you were allowed only one book to read in your lifetime and your choice was the Holy Bible, you would be not only happy and highly successful in this short life but have eternal life in paradise. Now that's *real* success. Read it now and every day and you'll find history repeating itself. In the book of Jeremiah written from 626-586 BC, you will find a theme which speaks to us today: *Failure to Repent Will Lead to Destruction.* Jeremiah saw that religion was essentially a moral and spiritual relationship with God, a relationship that required the devotion of each individual. Each person is responsible for his or her own sin. Through the centuries civilizations have risen and fallen, repeating again and again the errors of which Jeremiah warned. He prophesied to Judah's hard-hearted people during the reigns of four different kings. Is it any wonder he's called the weeping prophet? Will we never learn?

Dr. Harold L. Willmington of Liberty University writes in his book, *The King Is Coming,*

> *"The Decline and Fall of the Roman Empire* was written in 1788 by Edward Gibbon and set forth five basic reasons why the great civilization withered and died.

- The undermining of the dignity and sanctity of the home, which is the basis of human society.
- Higher and higher taxes; spending of public money for bread and circuses for the populace.
- The mad craze for pleasure; sports becoming every year more exciting, more brutal, more immoral.
- Building of great armaments when the real enemy was the decay of individual responsibility.
- The decay of religion; faith fading into mere form, losing touch with life and losing power to guide the people."

The phrase *History repeats itself* is an ominous warning in light of the above.

Dr. Willmington continues,

"The average age of the world's great civilizations has been 200 years. These nations progressed through this sequence:

From Bondage to Spiritual Faith
From Spiritual Faith to Great Courage
From Great Courage to Liberty
From Liberty to Abundance
From Abundance to Selfishness
From Selfishness to Complacency
From Complacency to Apathy
From Apathy to Dependence
From Dependence Back Again to Bondage"

Here we see the mirror image of America and the need to return to Religious Faith or die. I ask again, Will we ever learn? No, unless we study God's Word. If we do not trust in God, what are we saying? We are telling God we have a better idea and refuse to humble ourselves before our maker. Yes, America may die, but as individuals we do not have to die with her. God has promised us the opportunity for eternal life.

A comic actor, who led a sinful life, was dying in the hospital. A visiting friend found him reading the Bible and asked,

"What are you doing reading the Bible?"

The actor replied, "I'm looking for loopholes."

There is no loophole for the incorrigible sinner. Your repentance must come from your heart of hearts. Don't ignore the opportunity of your lifetime.

Jesus said, "I am the way, the truth and the life. No one comes to the Father but by me." Don't call Jesus a liar. He also said, "When you have seen me you have seen the Father."

I have written this book in the hope that you will pause and ponder your own personal destiny. I leave you with this truth. You were put here to make a choice. There's a reservation for you in heaven, but to avoid cancellation you must claim it now before it's too late. Remember, Jesus is the only ticket master—there is no other way.

RESOURCES

Bennett, William J. and John T. E. Cribb. *The American Patriot's Almanac*. Nashville, TN: Thomas Nelson, Inc, 2008

Federer, William J. *America's God and Country*. St. Louis, MO.: *Amerisearch, Inc., 2000.*

Holy Bible, NIV, Zondervan, 1984

Spirit-Filled Bible, NKJ version. Nashville TN.: Thomas Nelson, Inc., 1991.

Willmington, Harold. *The King Is Coming*. Carol Stream. IL.: Tyndale House Publishers, 1973.

Wilson, Don. *The Antibiotic an Ailing America Needs.* Bloomington, IN.: WestBow Press, 2012

Wilson, Don. *Code Name: WILLIAM TELL*. Bloomington, IN.: WestBow Press, 2013.

Wilson, Neil S, ed. *The Handbook of Bible Application*. Carol Stream, IL,: Tyndale House Publishers, 2000.

CPSIA information can be obtained at www.ICGtesting.com
Printed in the USA
BVOW01*1903040514

352329BV00003B/30/P